Mall Child

Greg Dunn

Dedication

This book is specifically dedicated to my Great-Aunt Katherine (Kate) Coyne Affleck. I never had the pleasure of knowing her since she died one year after my birth. However, I heard all about her. She took on the responsibility of raising my mother and her three brothers when their parents died while they were children. She assumed this responsibility on top of raising her own two children AND managing a business after her husband died prematurely. All of this after emigrating from Ireland to assimilate in America.

Beyond acknowledging Aunt Kate's fortitude, I dedicate the book to persons from all backgrounds and cultures who step up to the plate, making sacrifices, and doing what must be done. To all persons who get up early, work late, work their hardest, and fulfill their potential. Here's to all persons who do what's best for them and their families. Keep up the good work and don't give up.

Author Note

A word of caution, an explanation
and a call to action

The dialogue and content in this novel may be offensive or unsettling to some. There are events, situations, and circumstances that may be unsettling to others.

Ideas expressed by some characters that may be too outlandish or depressing to some. Reading about certain ideas and occurrences might cause you some discomfort, and that's normal. I'd be more worried if it didn't. Thinking outside-the-box and refusing to accept the hatred, racism, and cynicism that permeates our polarized society may actually be a prescription for change for the better.

So read on and be the change agent that's desperately needed. If at any point, the discomfort starts to feel overwhelming, please put the book down. Take care of yourself. You can always come back to it if you choose to.

If in need of counselling, guidance or resources in the USA, contact the National Alliance on Mental Illness (NAMI) at 1-800-950-6264 or helpline@nami.org

Chapter 1:
Christmas Eve Fight,
Christmas Eve Birth

Christmas Eve at the mall is the worst day of the year. Panicked procrastinating shoppers, merchants desperately trying to meet quotas. Youngsters anxiously awaiting St. Nick's visit only to be met by a two-hour line. For Joe Callahan, the mall's oldest cop, the day was filled with vehicle jump starts, food spills in the food court, and reuniting darlings with frantic parents. Putting on his uniform that morning, he knew he was in for a rough day. He had no idea what was in store for him.

As the 6:00 p.m. mall closing approached, the hustle and bustle turned violent when colors triggered a fight a scant twenty feet away from Santa's Village.

A female dispatcher's voice crackled on the two-way radios. "All units, ten–thirty-four reported at Santa's Village. All units copy, double time."

"Ho, ho, ho, here we go!" shouted Callahan, wolfing down the last bite of his ham and cheese sandwich, leaving a touch of mustard on his mustache.

"Whatever happened to peace on Earth, good will to men?" shouted back Wheeler, almost slide tackling Callahan as both guards exited the break room.

"Keeping alive the Christmas spirit with a good old Irish bar fight," wheezed Callahan as both guards slowed their pace, exiting the service corridor and entering the plaza full of shoppers or, as the mall cops called them, "civilians".

A teen from Norwood wearing a Crips necklace took a swing at a BellHaven teen wearing a Bloods bandanna. It was game on and over in a few seconds. Fists flew like on the set of the Jerry Springer Show.

"Break it up!" shouted Callahan to the teen in the Crips headband as he bobbed and weaved, unaware of Callahan's presence.

"Stay out of this, mall cop," snarled the kid.

"Step away from Santa and the kids," yelled Wheeler to the wannabe Blood in his red bandanna.

"Mall cops suck! You disrespect us," barked the indignant Blood, claiming he was just "foolin' with his cousin".

"They're the ones fighting but we're being disrespectful, go figure," muttered Callahan to himself.

"Show's over, let's move on, people," said Callahan in his best mall cop voice, smiling to himself and recalling how many times he used that expression.

One teen asked, "Why are you picking on me? I didn't do nothin'."

The other teen shouted, "He's nothin' but racist 'cause we're black." Callahan took a deep breath and explained in his best professional voice that fighting detracts from shopping.

Callahan patiently explained that, "In our capitalist system where the dollar is king, miscreants cannot be tolerated." This young man's banning was a street level lesson in the laws of economics, where the supply of shoppers goes down in direct proportion to the demand for crime. When Mr. Crip seemed perplexed by the economics lesson and the use of the word "miscreant" Callahan knew it was time to cut to the chase. That's when he told him, "Stay the fuck away from the mall for one year. If you come back, you'll be arrested for criminal trespass." This, he understood.

"Let's all wait by the doorway for Santa's elves to arrive," said Callahan, switching gears to the cheeriest voice he could muster. "Ah, here they come now. Look at them, all dressed in navy blue, carrying tasers and handcuffs," Callahan announced.

"Hey, Wheeler, get basic info from these mutts. The usual name, address, phone number. Probably all fake but we'll stick it in the report later. I gotta get away from these clowns before I lose my Irish temper."

"You got it," said Wheeler, recognizing Callahan's surface humor masked his slow burn of disgust with the ignorant and the insolent.

As usual with such skirmishes, nobody wanted to file charges. Both were charged with breach of peace and sent on their way. Angry young teens were released into the custody of equally angry family members with murmurs of retribution. There was unfinished business to be completed another day at hopefully a different location.

"My Christmas wish is that there's payback off-site," said Callahan.

"Hey, if there's enough payback, maybe it'll thin out the herd," said Wheeler.

Callahan frowned but let that comment slide, opting instead to exclaim, "Silent night, holy night."

Callahan had been on the force over fifteen years. His longevity is attributed to several reasons. He lived only a block from the mall. He only worked weekends so burnout was avoided. He worked two other jobs which kept him busy the rest of the week. Believe it or not, he actually felt rejuvenated by the time the weekend rolled around. By Friday night, he was ready to deal with knuckleheads. He had four kids, a mortgage, and car payments. In sum, he was a trapped, aging, white, working-class male.

Was he bitter? Hell no. A healthy dose of Irish wit and an underlying belief in the goodness of mankind (despite its blemishes) kept him upbeat in spite of personal setbacks and interactions with delinquents.

During the first six years of his "weekend warrior" shifts, friends and family used to act surprised to hear that he was still working the weekend gig. Their imperviousness to his dire financial circumstances initially got under his skin. Over time, he adapted by responding sarcastically, "I've got to keep myself busy. There's only so much time I can spend on my yacht."

At Callahan's weekday office job, coworkers always asked that perky Friday afternoon question, "So what are you doing this weekend?"

Callahan's response was always, "I work the three to eleven shift Friday, Saturday, and Sunday."

Eventually coworkers avoided the weekend plans question. They learned to avert eye contact. Being around Callahan on Friday afternoons was like being in the company of someone who has just informed you of a tragic event and you're at a loss for words.

Corporal Wheeler was half the age of Callahan and young enough to be his son. Youth and optimism usually go hand in hand. Not for Wheeler. He had a morbid view of humanity. He had good reason to view the glass as only half empty. His parents moved out of state. He didn't talk much about them. There was a sense that their relationship was fractured at best.

Wheeler, like many of his generation, dabbled with college while accumulating massive debt but coming up short on credits. He had a sister, and details of the story are vague, but essentially the sister's college expenses were covered at the expense of Wheeler's college dreams. Sort of a modern-day version of *Sophie's Choice*. Because of the need to finance college and a profuse sense of patriotism in the post-9/11 era, Wheeler joined the Army Reserve.

His specialization was community development. The mission of his unit was to "win the hearts and minds of third-world citizens in the hopes of turning them into staunch allies of the USA". This branch of the army might seem an odd fit for the sometimes-melancholy Wheeler. Deep down he had a strong sense of how international relations worked. In other circumstances and with the right financing, he could have been a prime candidate for the renowned Georgetown University School of Foreign Service as an international relations major. Wheeler had a bright, intuitive mind and a passion for history, particularly military history. That's why Callahan and Wheeler got along so well, sharing stories of historic and military trivia.

Back in the security office, Callahan removed his black Kevlar gloves. Wheeler sipped coffee as they wrote the report describing the fistfight. It included the usual who, when, what, and where. They completed so many of these reports they could do them in their sleep. As Callahan savored a Boston cream donut, he taunted Wheeler with the comment, "How's that cardboard taste?" Wheeler was glumly munching on a gluten free rice cake. He was repenting from the prior day's binging on a combination of Slim Jims and gummy bears. With the report completed, they reverted to their favorite pastime, testing each other's knowledge of history. Callahan asked Wheeler, "Who delivered the final blow to the Roman Empire?"

Wheeler hesitated to respond, letting Callahan think he stumped him. He then confidently stated, "Barbarian leader Odoacer, who swept down from northern Europe." It was a rare day when Callahan caught Wheeler flat footed concerning wars and revolutions. Imagine that, two mall cops, one eating healthy, having a discussion about the decline of the Roman Empire.

It's standard procedure for mall cops to be paired up after fights.

"Every fight seems to trigger another fight. Gets everybody hepped up," complained Wheeler. "Why aren't these kids home studying for their SATs?"

"Because this is America, not China," said Callahan. "Our kids only know how to party. They have no idea of what's around the corner. They'll never survive Armageddon."

With that ominous observation, the dispatcher's tired but professional voice announced over the radio, "Teens on cameras heading toward the family restroom."

Callahan lumbered down the service corridor with keys jingling on his black service belt and his two-way radio bouncing in his holster. Wheeler kept pace while managing to finish texting a girl in the hopes of meeting up for drinks at the end of the shift.

"No kids in here," quickly and casually announced Wheeler upon entry to the family restroom. "Must have gone to the food court instead."

"Thank God," said Callahan. "But let's sweep the area for love birds."

The family restroom was a magnet for teens looking to cuddle or cause trouble or both.

"Hey, what idiot splashed red paint on the black and white floor tiles?" said Callahan, shaking his head.

"Dude, that's blood, not paint. Check out the bloody tissues leading to the handicapped stall," said Wheeler as he took a few steps backward toward the exit doorway. Wheeler hung back, prodding Callahan, saying, "You go first."

Wheeler's specialty was fighting. He brought a skill set of mixed martial arts to the mall cop force. His athletic physique coupled with kicking and grappling skills mastered in army training was a reason they hired him. He was always ready to rumble but medical incidents made him squeamish.

"OK, chicken shit," said Callahan as he gingerly pushed open the stall door with his flashlight and shouted, "Holy shit, there's a baby in here."

A motionless but breathing newborn was wrapped in a blood-soaked blanket, so soaked that the original color was indiscernible.

Wheeler shouted over his radio, "Baby on floor next to the toilet." He forgot all about codes required when reporting incidents. Actually, no code was ever assigned for an incident of this sort.

Time stood still for Callahan and Wheeler, when in reality two shift supervisors arrived within a minute, cops within five minutes, the ambulance crew one minute later. Prompt emergency responses are a perk of living in a first world society. This was no ordinary call. All responders exhibited tunnel vision, focusing upon keeping the baby alive. The area was cordoned off just like on an episode of *Law & Order*. Every member played their position like a well-trained football team. EMS checked vitals and suctioned fluids, cops took pictures, dusted for prints, and summoned detectives for what would become a more extensive investigation.

Mall cops did what they were told to do. Observe, report, and reassure lingering patrons and employees that everything was OK. In reality, everything was not OK. It was Christmas Eve, when families are supposed to gather around the hearth sharing good cheer. Yet here was a baby, crying (thankfully), abandoned next to a toilet. Even baby Jesus had a mom and dad, some shepherds, and a motley crew of farm animals hanging around him. Mall Baby had no one.

It took less than an hour for word of the "mall birth" to spread far and wide, thanks to cell phones and social media. Soon, news crews arrived to cover this heart wrenching story on the most holy of nights. Mall management and security offered the customary, "No comment until a formal statement could be prepared."

Mall Baby was whisked off to St. Andrews Hospital. Fortunately, DCF (Department of Children and Families) was directed to the hospital in anticipation of taking the child into their custody. Referring to a human being who is less than two hours old as being in "custody" seems incredulous. Mall Baby did nothing wrong, but with all this hoopla of sirens, it seemed like he was already well on his way to a life of crime.

Chapter 2:
Postpartum Blues

It was past midnight when Callahan fumbled as he inserted his key into the wobbly doorknob of his front door.

"You'd think they'd leave the porch light on for old Callahan," he cussed to himself. "And why the hell do they lock the deadbolt above the doorknob? This dump is so run down, the burglars are gonna figure it's abandoned."

Callahan's wife, Maggie, and four kids were already asleep. Nobody to talk to about the most disturbing shift of his fifteen-year career. Settling into an overstuffed armchair, he cracked open a Guinness and watched a *Seinfeld* rerun.

Seinfeld was his favorite comedy, always providing a chuckle at the end of the day. Not so tonight. The image of a tiny hand protruding from that bloody blanket was seared into his mind. With the final sip of stout, his eyelids grew heavy and the *Seinfeld* episode ended. The show provided white noise to numb his racing mind.

As the TV screen blurred and the Guinness took effect, Callahan drifted into a sweet and sour dream. There was a little girl in denim overalls sporting a Dutch bob haircut, playfully wrestling with a terrier who refused to relinquish a dirty rag. The terrier was snapping his neck back and forth until the little girl got called to dinner by a husky older woman in a threadbare housecoat. Her face was indistinguishable but she exuded a mixed blend of firmness and concern. Callahan roused from the dream realizing that he had to pee. En route to the bathroom, he realized that the little girl was his mother and the stern caretaker was the girl's aunt. The aunt that adopted the six-year-old girl and her older brothers when their parents died.

As Callahan flushed the toilet, he wondered aloud, "Who will be the aunt for the baby that crossed my path this evening?

"Can't keep thinking of this or I'll be up all night. Got to get back to sleep. Big day tomorrow."

There was much to do on Christmas Day. Church to attend and relatives to visit before returning to the mall for the 3:00 p.m. shift. At least the mall would be closed so it would be a light shift, or so he thought.

When Wheeler got home he was greeted by Bear, his German shepherd. He was given that name because Wheeler's favorite show was *Person of Interest*. Bear was the East German shepherd that protected the two main characters, Mr. Finch (a computer geek type) and Mr. Rees (a 007-type character). Wheeler's purchase of a shepherd and naming him Bear reflected his admiration for the 007 character. He even bore a resemblance to Mr. Reese. The shepherd, the physicality, coolness under pressure, and the aloofness of a loner matched the persona of both Mr. Reese on TV and Mr. Wheeler in the mall.

Wheeler was relieved to be working Christmas Day at 3:00 p.m. There was no particular need to visit family. Exchanging presents was a distant memory from a long-lost truncated childhood. Wheeler wished for nothing more than to give himself and Bear a workout. Attending next week's army drill would give Wheeler the structure he needed and the camaraderie that he craved. Every reunion included stories where each soldier tried to outdo each other's story. Wheeler knew that the discovery of the baby would top all other stories. However, he thought, I'll only mention the fistfight I broke up between gangsters. There was something just too intense about discovering the baby that he could not bring himself to vocalize. For the first time in his young life, he appreciated how vets who saw action deferred talking. Wheeler experienced something very visceral that he knew would be his companion for a very long time.

Chapter 3:
It's a Wonderful Life

As soon as Callahan arrived for the 3:00 p.m. shift, conversations with Corporal Wheeler and dispatcher Wendy were abuzz with questions and reflections. Wendy asked while nervously tapping her favorite Winnie the Pooh pen, "Who's the mom? Why did she do it?"

Wheeler sheepishly divulged some inside information saying, "I friended Ms. Kim of the Asian Nail Salon some time ago on Facebook. Thought I might get lucky but then she got pregnant."

While looking over Wheeler's shoulder as the group was hunkered over Ms. Kim's Facebook page, Callahan chimed in, "That's the hot-looking Asian girl."

Wheeler and Wendy groaned, ignoring old Callahan's comment the way you shrug off your crazy uncle's jokes at the Thanksgiving dinner table.

Between incessant calls from patrons asking, "Is the mall open today?" Wendy exclaimed, "Now it all makes sense! Some months ago (nine, to be exact), Flash was hanging around the Asian Salon. Ms. Kim used to party harty. Now this explains why she recently said she was busy whenever we talked about going out clubbing."

"Flash, what an asshole." said Callahan, wringing his hands.

"Yea," said Wheeler, "didn't we ban him from the mall because he was threatening Ms. Kim? Didn't the shop manager want him removed?"

"That's the guy," affirmed Callahan as he pulled up his banning form from the computer. "Flash was definitely not the fatherly type. Impregnator, yes, but father, no."

"So what about Flash the rooster?" asked Wheeler. "Think he might step up to the plate?"

"Fat chance of that happening. He may not even know about the baby," scoffed Wendy. "Last I heard, he was doing time in Sommers for armed robbery."

Wendy sank back in her chair, letting customer calls go to the answering machine. "She ran out of options," said Wendy, tightening her blonde ponytail as she always did before launching into a tirade. "Can't have an abortion, they closed that door a few years back. Got a restraining order against Flash, but good luck relying on that. Remember that girl found dead in the park last year? She was clutching her goddamned restraining order."

"What about other Kims? You know, the whole extended family thing. Where the hell are they?" said Callahan, searching for some solution.

"Here's the deal," said Wendy, drawing in a deep breath. "No family. Not even a country to call home. She was Korean but now there's no Korea. Only a nuclear wasteland. I wish I knew all this sooner. Maybe I could have helped her somehow."

"So she was all alone here, saving money, and it was all good until the baby arrived. Was that the deal?" asked Wheeler, trying to get his head around her situation.

"Ms. Kim was very upset that her green card expired," explained Wendy. "She was facing deportation. Mentioned her broken English was holding her back from getting another job where she could make more money. I listened to her on lunch breaks but didn't think much more about it. If only I knew about the baby," said Wendy in a hushed, remorseful tone.

"Don't beat yourself up. Babies change everything. Take it from me. I had four of them," said Callahan, trying to lighten things up.

"I thought if she had a baby, that would keep her in this country? Couldn't the baby automatically become a US citizen? I even wonder if she had the baby just to stay in the USA," asked Wheeler who was still trying to figure out this Rubik's cube of birthing and citizenship.

Callahan reminded Wheeler, "Those laws changed. Both mom and child would now be deported. Unless," he mused, stroking his mustache, "some guardian angel appeared on behalf of the baby. There used to be a time when times get tough, the tough get going. Since the big crash, you know what's the new mantra?" asked Callahan.

"Tell us, Professor Callahan, what's the new world order," teased Wheeler.

"It's every man for himself. Everybody else gets kicked off the life raft. Shut the door behind you, not in my backyard, and damn the torpedoes," declared Callahan in a rant that Wendy and Wheeler knew by heart.

That's when all three members of this skeleton crew working on Christmas Day glanced at the clock.

"We have to look like we're working. This place is loaded with cameras," warned Callahan. Wendy took the phone calls off the answering machine and Wheeler shuffled off to conduct a round. Getting back to the mundane work routine offered relief from the emotional roller coaster of the past twenty-four hours. But the recurring thought that Callahan was right nagged them. Maybe we really are going to hell in a handbasket in a dog-eat-dog world.

As Callahan ambled down the service corridors, his knees occasionally creaked while making sure doors were locked. His mind chat of the prior day's event was interrupted by a call from Superman. Not the man of steel from outer space. Instead, he was a former mall cop from BellHaven who was now a corrections officer. Most people avoid jail but it was the perfect job for him.

Superman got his nickname even though his real name was Gabriel. Growing up tough in BellHaven, kicking everyone's ass in fights earned him the title Superman. While on the force at the mall, he was always challenging coworkers to hand wrestling contests. His sausage-like fingers had the crushing power of a jackal's jaw tearing apart a carcass. Nobody wanted to be the carcass. Beneath this fierceness, Superman had a heart of gold and a sense of right over wrong. He heard about the discovery of the baby since it was all over the news. Since

Superman had a cousin who worked as a nurse in St. Andrews Hospital, he also knew that foster care arrangements were getting underway.

Callahan nonchalantly mentioned, "Well that's good, the kid should be OK."

Superman was quick to correct him. "Everybody thinks foster care is cool. Like it's one-and-done. Out of sight, out of mind. Well, let me tell you, it's the beginning of the end for that kid."

Callahan countered, "Maybe he'll be placed in a nice house with a nice family. You know, a real Norman Rockwell scene like something out of the movie *It's a Wonderful Life*."

"Dream on," said Superman. "Let me tell you the real deal. The kid's gonna be shuttled from house to house at best. At worst, he's destined to a life of abuse. I should know. I was bounced around till age ten when Uncle Festus intervened."

"All these years working with you, I never knew that," sheepishly admitted Callahan. "We work shifts together and share mall tales. We don't know the shit that happened to us before joining the force. Deep down we're all Irishmen. We're masters of compartmentalization."

"Yea, well now you know. Uncle Festus was a heavy drinker. He wasn't really an uncle. He was my parents' drinking buddy. He kicked the habit and they kicked the bucket. That's why we need to do something," said Superman with a shortness of breath that accompanies painful honesty.

"You may be Puerto Rican but you could have been Irish," quipped Callahan. "You got all the ingredients: alcohol, tragedy, recovery."

"Are any of us really all that different? All we really have is each other. And this baby needs us," said Superman with a laser focus.

Callahan perked up at his end of the phone call., "What do you mean 'we' and what the hell are you talking about?"

"I'm talking about not letting this kid get lost in the system."

"Well at least here there's a system," retorted Callahan. "In other countries, it's called infanticide. The Great Crash ripped away whatever safety net existed."

Superman forged onward, "There's a reason she left the baby in such a public place. She knew you guys make regular rounds. She knew he would not be left alone for long."

Silence on Callahan's end of the line was Superman's cue to present his final argument. "There's another reason we all have to step up to take care of this baby."

"Oh yea, and what's that?" asked Callahan, not sure he wanted to know the answer.

"Don't you find it ironic that the baby was discovered on Christmas Eve by a couple of guys who are part of a much larger family?"

Callahan could see where Superman was going. He "found Jesus" a few years ago and viewed the world through a religious lens. Oh boy, here we go, thought Callahan, as Superman insisted it was fate that brought this child into their lives. Superman was convinced it was destiny in the making and they were called to do the right thing.

"So I suppose we're the shepherds or the wise men. Maybe we're just the donkey and the oxen in that Christmas fantasy," said Callahan sarcastically. Callahan thought often about big issues such as heaven and hell, good versus evil, and the meaning of life. However, he strayed from formal religion and drifted toward existentialism after years in a grinding routine of eat-sleep-work. Superman remained undeterred in his zeal for what he now called the "second rescue of Mall Baby".

Second rescue sounds way too much like the Second Coming that Superman so often harped about with anyone who would listen, thought Callahan. Let him unravel and preach, thought Callahan as he gritted his teeth and tensed his jaw, ending the conversation with, "We'll see."

At roll call on the day after Christmas, Big Jack the security director issued the usual warning announcing, "This is the most dangerous day of the year for mall cops." Thanks to social media and a steady erosion of the moral compass of America's youth, this day at malls all across America became a day of wilding. Flash mobs rampaged, causing maximum chaos in minimum time. Peace on Earth and good will to men on the prior day was a distant memory. This year was no exception with batches of unruly youths shouting and running through the mall, causing mayhem. At the conclusion of the shift, when Big Jack thanked his troops for staying professional throughout the chaos, he waxed sentimental in light of the discovery of Mall Baby on Christmas Eve. Beneath the hard-ass veneer that's a job description for security directors, the barrel chested, broad shouldered Big Jack told his crew he feared for the future of this child in light of today's experience. Years of working at this job made him a "glass half empty" sort of guy. He wondered aloud if this child would grow up in a world when every day would resemble *The Purge* rather than the movie version of the one-day Purge. After a day of being called blue-eyed white devils and mother fuckers, the crew went home wondering what the future held not only for the baby but for each other.

Chapter 4:
What's in a Name?

The chart affixed to the crib in the hospital nursery was bureaucratically labeled "Baby B". Why? He was a boy, the only baby boy delivered on Christmas Eve. Swaddled in the customary blue blanket with the pale blue cap pulled over his head, he arrived healthy and nameless.

Two baby girls were born that evening. Their bassinets already tricked out with heart shaped balloons, red roses, and plenty of pink knickknacks. Their names were Samantha and Sabrina and an entourage of families excitedly kept watch over them from behind the observation window.

When news of the mall birth hit the airways, broadcasters simply identified him as Mall Baby. Ratings went through the roof.

Meanwhile, back at Burpees Diner, Callahan, his kids (Bryce, Claire, Kevin, and Bruce), and a gaggle of mall cops hunkered over fried chicken and ribs on the day after national mall riot day.

"I'm exhausted," exclaimed Callahan as the group pulled together tables in the corner, enabling them quick access to the bathrooms and clear view of the entrance.

"I'm not sure how many more years I can work on national mall riot day."

"I'm not sure how many more years America can stand this. Kids running wild, acting feral," said young Wheeler with the air of a man closer to retirement age.

The mall cops regrouped and rested after mayhem experienced on the day after Christmas. They lounged like soldiers taking respite after a hard-fought battle. Normally during Christmas break Bryce would be on his high school senior year ski trip. Twins Claire and Kevin would be at the ice rink practicing for the upcoming ice capades. They were known locally as the dynamic duo in teen tournaments. A recent snowfall brought sheer delight for Bruce, who would have been sledding with middle school friends on a steep hill located on the other side of the mall.

But this was no ordinary Christmas break. Serious conversations were needed and decisions had to be made.

Gabriel (a.k.a. Superman) was still on his soapbox, campaigning for a safety net for the baby. "We can't change America but we can make a difference in that child's life," said Gabriel, waving the menu as if it was a cue card in a political debate.

Ever the pragmatist, Callahan declared, "Let's start with the basics. The child needs a name! He can't grow up being called Mall Baby. Eventually, he'll be called Mall Child and then what'll we call him … Mall Man? Tarzan started out being called 'boy' and somehow got named Tarzan. See how the right name can get you far in life?"

Ralph, still groggy from working two back-to-back shifts at the mall, asked, "How did he go from being 'boy' to Tarzan?" Even when Ralph was alert, he tended to get off topic. He was a burly guy with a rough exterior but a heart of gold. Sort of like a well-worn work glove with a soft knit lining.

"Forget about the Tarzan story, we can't worry about that right now," shrugged Callahan as the waitress re-filled mugs. "We gotta focus on getting this kid a name, every other baby has a name."

Claire insisted that the only name they should con-sider is Jesus. "Do I have to remind you heathens of the date he was born?"

Callahan experienced a flashback to nuns in grammar school, Xaverian Brothers in high school, and graduation from the Catholic University of America. In this mo-ment of religious PTSD, he exclaimed, "I don't mean to run up against the big guy but there are atheists that might get pissed off by this."

"You want him to grow up commanding respect and kicking some ass," said Junior. "Well I got just the right name."

Now Junior with his mohawk haircut and serpent tat-toos on both forearms was known for some strange ideas. Some questioned whether he belonged to this planet. He was the first to claim that mass shootings were figments of an overreaching media. He was among the misguided band of Holocaust deniers.

"Yea, what?" said Callahan wearily.

"We should name him Hitler 'cause maybe he can finish what the great one started."

"Let's all just drink some of Junior's Kool Aid," said Big Jack. Junior took the cue but continued to scroll for kernels of misinformation among his favorite newsfeeds.

Big Jack was no flaming liberal and he was not a warm and fuzzy guy when it came to social justice. But he knew right from wrong and never missed an opportunity to let Junior know when his head was up his ass.

Corporal Wheeler couldn't resist a discussion involving history, particularly military history. He suggested the name Attila. "It's perfect. The kid is half Asian, so a Mongolian surname fits. He's gonna have to kick some ass since this world is getting crazier by the moment."

"You got that right," chimed in Butch and Ralph, never missing opportunities for negative prognostication.

"If he moves to the plains of the Midwest, he'll be right at home riding horses and rounding up cattle," declared Wheeler. "I can see him now, firing AR-15s in the air, scaring off liberal bastards who try to set up shop out there."

Wheeler was quite the anomaly. The branch of the army he joined was known within the service as the Peace Corp, filled by peaceniks masquerading as soldiers trying to make the world a better place. Globally he was a liberal but domestically he was quite conservative. Go figure.

"I'm OK with Attila. It has a cultural connection," said Callahan. "Wheeler, you always grasp the arc of history."

"I've learned from the best," said Wheeler, reaching for ketchup to smother his fries.

"However," cautioned Callahan, "someday Attila will be interviewing for a job and this name might be a drag on his career. How many kids do you know named Hitler or Attila? Even the most badass kids from our child-hoods didn't have those names."

Silence descended on this normally raucous group.

Burpees Diner was one of those silver-clad, retro greasy spoon joints where the waitresses always seem tired and the prices somehow remained reasonable. Every booth still had one of those glass-encased juke-boxes where you could turn the pages to choose your favorite musical selections. For fifty cents you could be transported back to the innocence of the 1960s when songs had meaning and you could hear the words. No wonder Callahan loved this place. As Sammy Davis belted out his song "I've Got To Be Me", Callahan ex-claimed, "That's it!"

"What's it?" responded twins Claire and Kevin, thinking he had dropped something on the floor.

"Sammy Davis. It's the perfect name for Mall Baby."

Callahan was met with blank stares so he knew some explaining was needed. "First of all, we go with a name like Sammy because it's friendly. It's not rough and in your face like 'Ralph' or 'Butch', no offense, guys."

"None taken," mumbled Butch with a mouth full of fries as he reached for extra pickles for his burger. Butch was frequently mistaken for Ralph. Both sported cop-hair crew cuts, receding hairlines, and expanding waist-lines. Their routines outside of work included alternating visits to the donut shop and the gym. They sauntered about town still wearing high school colors in ex-athlete physiques. They were not as limber as they used to be but years of tangling with knuckleheads at the mall painted them with a no-nonsense veneer that cried out "make my day" to those who challenged them verbally or physically.

Undeterred, Callahan continued to build his case. "Sammy's the kind of name that could go either way, maybe a boy or maybe a girl."

"And you think that's a good thing?" scoffed Butch whose interest was aroused by this boy–girl thing.

"Yea, get with the times. Sometimes you gotta play both sides of the fence. If this kid runs for office, he needs votes from wherever and whomever he can get 'em."

"The kid's only four days old and you got him running for President," quipped Ralph.

"It doesn't matter. The President's days are numbered. The revolution is coming. It'll be like the French and Russian Revolutions combined. Blood in the street, nothing to eat, and heads of the rich bastards rolling downhill," chimed in Junior.

"Somebody please cut off Junior from the Kool Aid," barked Big Jack.

"Now that we got the first name straight, we need a good last name, let's focus here, guys," said Callahan.

This was Superman's cue. After all, it was his idea to get Mall Baby adopted by mall cops and a gaggle of supporting cast members. "Wait a minute, I thought his last name would be Callahan since I thought you were adopting him?"

"Now you wait a minute, Mr. Big Ideas," retorted Callahan. "I'm only stepping up to this adoption thing if everybody else joins the bandwagon. And I really mean sign on. I can get my lawyer friend Bob to write up a nice contract that names me as the guardian but only if everybody else chips in with their time and talents. I'm just the guardian, not the dad, so he needs his own name."

"I see where you're going with this," mused Wheeler. "So this would be like George Washington signing the Declaration of Independence but only if his crew also signs on to back him up."

"Thank you, Wheeler, for the history lesson, but yea, that's the gist of it."

"So are we all in on this … yes or no?"

The silence was broken only by an uneasy fidgeting with utensils and clinking of glasses. One by one, everyone at the table that day at Burpees Diner said yes to stepping up.

"So back to the naming thing," said Callahan. "Are you all OK with the name Sammy Davis?"

Ralph's third cup of coffee kicked in and he needed a reminder of the significance of this particular name.

Callahan obliged, explaining that the original Sammy Davis was the only black member of a group known as the "Rat Pack". He was one of the first crossover entertainers when TV back in the 1960s was predominantly white oriented. Fellow members were Dean Martin, Frank Sinatra, Peter Lawford, and Joey Bishop. More blank stares from the younger generation at the table. So Callahan informed them that this was a group that hung out in Las Vegas, drank heavily, womanized, and made a ton of money. For the crew assembled at Burpees Diner, this sealed the deal. Everyone connected with the notion of being part of a group known as the Rat Pack.

After the craziness of the holiday had passed, mall cops traditionally gathered the weekend after New Year's at a watering hole down the street in BellHaven to blow off steam. In the Latino-Christian culture, this time of year is called Little Christmas. Legend has it that three wise men arrived bearing gifts. Flash forward to contemporary times and mall cops euphemistically called this gathering "choir practice". Modern-day gift giving consisted of buying drinks and playing pool. Superman told Callahan that he and some other members of the mall cop alumni would attend this gathering and float his proposal of doing what's right for the baby. Superman was big on ideas and enthusiasm but short on details.

Superman was a man with a plan. He kickstarted the conversation recanting the night in Willy's Water Hole on St. Patrick's Day when Callahan was loaded up on Guinness and got sentimental telling about his mom.

"Oh, I see where you're going now, playing the mom card," said Callahan. "So what did I say?"

"You told us about how your mom and her three brothers were raised by their Aunt Kate because her parents died young. You said Aunt Kate came over from Ireland with a thick Irish brogue. She joined her husband and already had two kids of her own," said Superman.

Quietness descended on this motley group. Everyone enjoyed a story, especially if it got juicy, sad, or violent.

"Go on," instructed Callahan. "Tell me more about my family roots."

"Well, Aunt Kate's husband started a moving company with a horse and wagon and it was doing OK but then he died suddenly of a heart attack. You said that Aunt Kate not only kept the business running but she expanded it to the point where they were running moving trucks up and down the East Coast. She was a woman running a company in the 1920s with a strong Irish brogue when it wasn't cool to be Irish. What's that term they used for that back then?"

"It was NINA, meaning No Irish Need Apply," said Butch who prided himself for knowing all things Irish.

"I'll also let you know that Aunt Kate ran a rooming house," added Callahan. "She took in Irish immigrants helping them get their first job. She made cash on the side. Helping others while helping herself. We don't do that anymore. Nowadays with all our toys, we don't realize we're all alone until it's too late."

"Whatever happened to rooming houses?" asked Ralph. "I lived in them, saving up to buy my first house. Like the rest of you house poor suckers, now I'm living paycheck to paycheck."

"Superman, you've got a great memory. But what's my ancient family history got to do with this baby?" asked an increasingly impatient Callahan.

"Connect the dots," said Superman. "We're living here in a modern-day version of your mom and your uncles."

"You got me there," said Callahan, stroking his mustache and stirring his coffee. He switched over to coffee, sensing that big decisions were about to be made and he needed to keep his wits about him.

"But I already got four kids of my own. One's entering college, two are in high school and one's in middle school. I'm working full time and doing this mall cop gig on weekends. I haven't had a weekend off for over fifteen years. I'll agree to this guardianship stuff, but I need all the mall cops to back me up, like when we back each other up during a fight."

"Count us in," said Ralph, banging his meaty palm on the table. "Plus we can teach the kid how to ride a bike, swim, and, of course, handle himself in a fight."

Butch added, "I can help out but remember I got kids and bills of my own."

Leaning forward with his elbows on the table, Ralph confided, "Marge has been in a deep funk lately. Her enlarged heart seems to be getting the better of her. That's why we never had kids. She needs more direction, more purpose in life."

"Sorry to hear that," said Callahan, making that rare eye to eye contact that men do when the topic veers into sickness or death. "You should have told us. Let us know if we can help in any way."

"Us Pollacks are like you Irish," said Ralph, leaning back in his chair trying to lighten up the conversation. "We keep a lid on our shit until it boils over."

Pushing around his half-eaten food and looking off into the distance, he added, "Maybe, just maybe, Marge could be this kid's nanny for the first couple of years till he's school age."

"With me and Maggie working full time, we're not around to raise him properly, at least for the first few years," said Callahan.

"I'll run it by Marge tonight. It's a big commitment but like I said, she's got a big heart in more ways than one."

Taking a deep breath, Callahan announced, "This is a big decision. I got to run this adoption or guardian thing by my lawyer buddy Bob. Let's sleep on it and regroup next Friday night."

"I hate to be a killjoy," said Wheeler, "but you realize that this kid's gonna have to play the Asian card and the Black card depending upon what knucklehead he's dealing with—and there's no shortage of knuckleheads."

Superman jumped to the rescue saying, "We're gonna teach him everything he needs to know, just like our ancestors cross-trained us. This kid's gonna get us back to the days when everybody was a mechanic, carpenter and fighter."

"Not like today," scoffed Ralph, "when we run off buying our own houses and acting like we don't know each other. We're all too good for each other. Everybody buys their own lawnmower and snow blower. Nowadays we just wave to each other thinking, 'see how I'm so neighborly'."

Sitting askew from the group and giving the evil eye to a raven perched on a tree branch outside the corner window, Junior announced, "The barbarians are heading our way. It's not just the feral kids at the mall."

"Kid, you made a good point for once," said Big Jack.

"Who are all these barbarians you guys keep talking about?" asked Claire.

Callahan jumped right in with his usual spiel describing terrorists, both foreign and domestic, supremacists, extremists, mass shooters, and regular shooters.

"Callahan, you're on your soap box again," said Wheeler. "Can we get back to this kid? How's he gonna explain us to his friends. Remember the show *The Munsters* on the Retro TV channel? Remember how there was that beautiful girl being raised by those misfit monsters. She was hot, what was her name?"

"It was Marilyn," said Butch, leaning into Wheeler's personal space, "but let's not get sidetracked with your teen fantasies. And are you calling us a bunch of misfit monsters?"

"Well, we are," said Wheeler. "Look at us. Blue collar losers working multiple jobs, living paycheck to paycheck while the rich hedge fund guys live off their investments. How exactly do those bastards make money out of nothing?"

"Leave the hedge fund boys alone. They're dead to me," said Callahan. "We gotta make sure this kid doesn't get lost in the system. Maybe we can just save one."

"One's a good start," said Ralph, clasping his hands together as if he was a minister leading the congregation in prayer.

And so it was that in the redneck recesses of Willy's Water Hole, the rescue plan for Mall Baby was hatched by Superman. Over pitchers of beer and handfuls of beer nuts, Superman slowly built a consensus of concern that he capped off with the soundbite, "Rednecks to the rescue." Objections raised by skeptics of his ambitious adoption plan were temporarily silenced by Superman's final question, "Who among us has not had somebody in their life they could depend on? Someone who loved them unconditionally?"

A cord had been struck that night. Everyone knew there would be no going back on this commitment. A life had to be rescued.

Chapter 5:
Who Rescued Who

The Callahan clan settled into a hectic but manageable routine. Eat-sleep-work and REPEAT. Prior to Sammy's arrival, their lives were vanilla with occasional sprinkles. World boundaries rarely expanded beyond workplaces, classrooms, and the monthly drumbeat of bill payments. Sammy changed all that. Those first few years when Sammy moved from the bassinet to the tricycle were a blur. Many years later, when Sammy was old enough to sit at the bar of Willy's Water Hole, he fondly reflected upon childhood experiences. With his left hand grasping a pint, he reminded Callahan that his ring finger still exhibited a scar caused when he plunged his hand through the glass window on a storm door.

Callahan groaned, "Do we have to relive that experience?"

Bar buddies Ralph and Butch acted like they didn't know the story and requested a recounting of it. They never tired of an opportunity to taunt Callahan.

Sammy obliged, stretching his long legs on a nearby chair recalling that, "Callahan was supposed to be putting me down for a nap. Instead he chased me around bellowing, 'boo-da temple,' making me believe he was a witch doctor with a towel slung over his head. I scampered away but didn't realize the storm door was locked. My little palm smashed through the glass pane."

"Owww!" said Butch and Ralph in unison, raising a toast to Callahan's tomfoolery.

"To this day, I remember that old white porcelain sink in the tiny bathroom adjacent to the kitchen brimming with red water. I was screaming while Callahan shoved my hand into that bloody whirlpool."

"You're just lucky I was a mall cop and didn't faint like the rest of this nation of namby pambies," retorted Callahan.

"You're just lucky Maggie didn't kill you when she found out what happened," said Butch.

"When she got home from pushing papers at her job at city hall, I was put in the doghouse for a couple of days. But, like they say, life goes on. What doesn't kill you makes you stronger," said Callahan whose patience was wearing thin with all this reminiscing.

Butch asked Sammy in the most condescending voice he could muster, "Do you want me to schedule an appointment with a therapist so you can express your innermost feelings about this traumatic incident? Maybe Callahan could also attend to iron out his guilt."

"Sign me up with the shrink. I could also tell him about the day the training wheels came off my bright yellow Huffy bike," said Sammy.

"I remember that bike, you loved it. Especially when I customized it with that red, white, and blue banana seat. I made the mistake of adding that stupid bell which drove us all crazy," chuckled Ralph. "So what was the problem with the bike?"

"Nothing until the training wheels got taken off too soon by you guys. I thought I was OK, cruising on the brand new pavement in front of Aunt Genevieve's house, but when I hit the cracked slabs in front of Mrs. Chicarella's house, I went flying. It's funny how you never forget that childhood stuff," said Sammy.

"You were mad as a hornet," said Callahan. "I remember you coming into the house with bloody knees. You shouted, 'I hate this piece of shit. I'm never gonna ride it.' I gave you some distance and kept my eye on you. Just like I do with the knuckleheads at the mall. Let 'em vent a little so long as they don't hurt themselves or somebody else.

"I remember smiling to myself, thinking, Ralph and Butch are adding to his vocabulary."

"Hey, don't throw us under that bus. Maggie lectured us about forbidden words inside the house," said Ralph.

"You know," said Butch, leaning forward ominously toward Sammy, "you weren't the most coordinated kid on the block. As I recall, you were also the heftiest kid in the neighborhood."

"Oh, I see how this works," said Sammy. "Now it's my turn in the hot seat. Well let me tell you, the baby fat is long gone and it never came back."

"You got that right. Nobody beats you on the track and in the pool," said Callahan quickly and nonchalantly. For Callahan and clan members, tossing verbal jabs rolled easily off lips. Compliments were delivered sideways as afterthoughts when in reality they were serious, dead serious.

Chapter 6:
It Takes a Village…

The Fixer

The Callahan household provided a safe, warm, welcoming home for Sammy. There were always three hots and a cot, with the bare necessities. More importantly, there were lots of laughs and always a sense of place. He had a place to stay, a place to go, and a place to be loved. Not bad for a kid who started out abandoned on a bathroom floor. As supportive as this household was, there is only so much you can learn (both good and bad) from your immediate family.

To the rescue came the extended family known as Callahan & Company. They offered a menagerie of skills that even the largest of families could not provide. Case in point, Callahan was not mechanically inclined. The extent of his mechanical abilities stretched only as far as jumpstarting a car and replacing the roll on the toilet dispenser. Callahan's father was equally inept when it came to all things mechanical. His uncle Big Louie and his first cousin Little Louie were mechanics. Callahan always wished that more time could have been spent with them learning that trade.

Callahan frequently lamented, "If you can fix a car, you can always get somewhere. If you fix somebody else's car, you can make a quick buck on the side." Thanks to weekends spent with Uncle Stanley, a master mechanic, Sammy could distinguish a manifold from a carburetor and everything in between. Uncle Stanley's knack for improvising and making do with limited materials, earned him the nickname "MacGyver" in the extended family. He had pet names for auto parts. Transmissions were referred to as "trannies" and carburetors were "carbies". Uncle Stanley's fireplace mantel had the usual wedding photos and children's graduation pictures but they were interspersed with framed photos of his beloved Mustangs and Corvettes.

He was a patient mentor for Sammy under the hood and in the tool room. Sammy learned shortcuts never taught in trade school. Even if Sammy could not fix something, at least he could diagnose the problem. He didn't choose mechanics as his life profession but years later he thanked Uncle Stanley for giving him the confidence that comes from knowing how things work even if you can't fix 'em. This knowledge served him well when he joined the military in support of America's endless wars and what turned out to be America's endless recession. Belt tightening and making something out of nothing become as important as framed diplomas displayed on mantels.

<u>**The Fighter**</u>

Sammy's first several years were generally fun and uneventful. These are the years when kids can be kids, playing their hearts out. There was sledding in the winter and swimming in the summer. It wasn't until middle school when adult animosities encroached upon childhood innocence. The slightest differences in speech, appearance, or anything for that matter get picked up by those who like to pick on. Sammy was no exception. His mixture of Afro-Asian features coupled with his coffee complexion made him an easy target. His appearance on the playground attracted the attention of the regulars who started with the usual question, "Where you from?" Thinking locally, Sammy responded, "Northville."

The regulars laughed and scoffed saying, "No, stupid, I meant what country are you from?"

Sammy naively replied, "USA," to which they howled, "You must be from the Land of Gebba!" and they encircled him chanting, "Gebba, Gebba, I'm from the Land of Gebba."

Sammy went home that day confused and flustered. He didn't mention the experience to anyone, thinking it was a one-time event that would blow over.

It did not.

Next day, the regulars were back but today their questioning took a bitter turn.

The fat-assed, loud-mouthed ringleader asked point blank, "So what are you, a nigger or a chink?" Before the stunned Sammy could respond, one of his skinny, baseball capped henchmen commented, "Maybe he's a spic."

Sammy was surrounded but he was saved by the bell summoning the end of recess. Sammy had friends in school. He was not a wallflower. But the schoolyard code of silence is strong. Everybody from teachers to parents to TV commercials talk about "seeing something and saying something" but in the schoolyard jungle, the inclination is to keep a low profile and be glad they're not picking on you.

That night at dinner Sammy still made no mention of this disturbing exchange but he was clearly rattled by it and lost sleep over it. Seeing that he was not his playful self, Callahan asked, "How was school?" to which Sammy murmured, "OK." Uncle Ralph was visiting and knew something was bugging Sammy. Next day at the schoolyard, the regulars were back at it since they were having too much fun with their new patsy. They skipped the introductory insults and went straight to shoving Sammy back and forth among the three of them. Fat-ass delivered a punch, knocking Sammy to the ground. He went home that day with a black eye. There would be no more hiding his anguish. Uncle Ralph happened to be over for dinner at Callahan's as was his routine on Friday evenings. Maggie was serving fish and chips every Friday since this meatless Lent tradition in an Irish-Catholic household carried on throughout the year.

Uncle Ralph leaned forward, grabbing both a fish stick and a better look at Sammy, saying, "What the hell happened to you?"

"Nothin'," said Sammy, eyes downcast as he fidgeted with his fork.

"Doesn't look like nothin' to me," said Ralph.

"Three guys bothering me at school."

"Give me names, addresses," said Ralph as he eased back in his chair, lighting up a cigar like the character Sonny on *The Sopranos*. "Hey, Butch, what do you say we take a road trip?"

Butch had been watching a skinny, shirtless, toothless guy get wrestled to the ground on a *Live PD* episode. This was his favorite show. "Gets me in the right frame of mind to work a shift at the mall," he liked to say.

Butch managed to listen in on Sammy's schoolyard saga as the TV police dispatcher alerted a county sheriff somewhere down south that a domestic incident was brewing over a pack of cigarettes.

"I'm always up for squashing some snowflakes," said Butch as his attention shifted to Sammy's schoolyard scuffle.

Ralph pressed Sammy for details, "What did they say?"

"They called me a nigger, a chink, a spic bastard."

"Redneck assholes. Who do they think they are?" added Butch.

"Where's the Land of Gebba?" asked Sammy. "They say I'm from Gebba."

Butch said, "It's nowhere. It's made up. It's code for you come from somewhere else and you need to go back there."

Ralph said, "How about me and Butch do a stake out and jump 'em when they're alone, like we did in the old days."

Butch initially showed enthusiasm as he put down the barbell he used for curls during TV commercials. "On second thought," he said, "let's not go back to the old days."

Now Uncle Ralph was the guy you wanted on your side when picking sides for a fight. Legend had it, he was expelled on his first day of high school because he got into four fights. One on the bus going to school, one in his first class, one in the hallway, and one in the principal's office. Uncle Ralph was a scrapper all his life. He was more than happy to share with Sammy his street fighting techniques. He offered not only to go to school and kick their asses but to also hunt down their parents.

Callahan suggested a more moderate course of action. "Why don't you guys instruct Sammy in Krav Maga. It works for the Israeli army, so bring it to Northville. Spring break is next week. This will give you guys just enough time to train Sammy."

"We only got one week, but luckily there's only ten moves you got to learn. Perfect for street fighting. None of those fancy poses in Karate," said Butch.

"Yea, I don't trust any martial art where you wear a bathrobe to fight," scoffed Ralph.

"You moron, they call those bathrobes *gies* wrapped around with colored belts that are supposed to intimidate you," said Butch.

Ignoring Butch's correction, Ralph plunged onward scheduling the first workout for tomorrow at 10:00 a.m. He gave Sammy an encouraging pat on the back and issued a high five, telling him, "Your speed as a runner and your endurance as a swimmer would make you a kick-ass fighter."

"Thanks, guys," said a relieved Sammy. "I'm going to bed early so I'm ready for tomorrow's workout."

Once Sammy was safely out of earshot, Callahan lamented, "He gained too much weight during his early childhood years eating M&M candies at Aunts Agnes and Helen's house. They never married and never had kids so they over-indulged him. I wish I could have been around more for him but with Maggie and I working around the clock, that was not in the cards."

"Don't beat yourself up," cautioned Ralph. "Sammy's weight is down and his confidence is coming up. He's having the kind of childhood we had. We were free-roam chickens, playing to our hearts' content. He plays with neighborhood kids just like we did. Now that's a frigging lost art. Now they have to do commercials just to get kids to go outside."

"You're bringing back memories of good times," said Butch wistfully. "Lazy summer days riding ten-speed bikes from Northville down narrow highways to the beach for a swim. Sammy's lucky he has bike buddies Peter, Mark, and Billy."

"We used to bike anywhere and everywhere. No helmets and a little plastic water bottle attached to the bike frame. Now kids train for that race where you swim, run, and bicycle. What's the name of that race?" asked Ralph.

"It's called a triathlon. You want to join one this summer? There are triathlons for old guys like us. What do you say?" teased Butch. "You could wear a pink Speedo, if they have an extra-large size."

"Sign me up but don't wait for me," said Ralph with his fingers crossed behind his back.

By the end of spring break and a grueling routine, Sammy mastered ten fighting scenarios. When the school bus picked him up on Monday, his last words to Callahan were, "Let's do this!"

Callahan assisted with the boxing matches during the week in what little time he had running between his three jobs. Callahan made sure that practicing Krav Maga was conducted in the driveway on Sunday morning, Easter Sunday no less.

"Just one of life's little pleasures," he would frequently remark to Maggie. "Staging fights in front of the evangelical church across the street from our dump. Reminds me of the time I grabbed a pair of mannequin's legs from the mall and stuck them upside down in a snowbank."

"Or the time you stuck those legs in the back of our neighbor's pickup truck and asked his wife if she knew what he was up to on weekends," said Maggie, doing her best to act perturbed at Callahan's penchant for mischief.

"Shocking evangelicals and training Sammy to kick redneck ass, it doesn't get any better than this," said Callahan as he conducted a victory jig abbreviated by Maggie's admonition to, "Act your age and make sure you take the trash out tonight before pick up tomorrow."

In addition to the muscle memory of kicks and jabs, Sammy was armed with the confidence to defend himself. When recess rolled around on the first day back from vacation, Sammy was ready. Mr. Fat-ass sauntered up to him with a threatening gesture intending to make Sammy flinch. Rather than flinch, he delivered a spartan kick to his midsection, plunking his fat ass onto the pavement. His sneaky, skinny cohort approached from behind but Sammy clocked him as he thrust his right elbow backward into his face. This pointy nosed creep now sported a blood-soaked mustache. The third amigo ran for cover, realizing he was no match for Sammy who terminated his two bully friends in short order. As with every schoolyard fight, this one had its spectators and word of Sammy's surprise attack spread far and wide in the world of middle school. Sammy would have no further challenges until he stepped up to the bigger high school arena.

Chapter 7:
The Growing Years

Sammy adjusted well to school. More so than most kids because of play dates with youngsters affiliated with his extended family. Some of his mall cop uncles were raising families of their own. Their kids played tag, manhunt, and king of the hill with him every weekend. His uncles' calendars were full. That's why they could not take on the responsibility of raising Sammy full time. Callahan's household provided the optimum launch pad. His own four kids were at the upper end of the schooling ladder but not yet established in careers. Young enough to have youthful exuberance but old enough to contemplate how they could have better managed their formative years. For Sammy, they were the older, wiser, and yet still fun older brothers and sister.

Sammy's first years of grade school were filled with the typical activities of a public school student in suburban America. There was running to catch the school bus, deciding who to sit next to at lunch, and who to play with at recess. There were school plays and concerts where every child was cute even when some forgot their lines and sang off-key. The Christmas concert was always an emotional event. Not so much for Sammy since he had no recollection of his birth or the circumstances surrounding that fateful day. For him it was an evening of keeping your black tie straight and your nose from running. He and most of the choir were fighting the sniffles. The Christmas concert invariably struck a chord with the Callahan clan and Sammy's extended family. They made sure a representative was present at benchmark events in the young life of this child. While other families juggled calendars to attend events given their hectic work schedules and commuting patterns, there was never a shortage on Sammy's team given the depth of that team.

Since it had been several years since the widespread publicity of his birth on the bathroom floor, Sammy's presence in school was inconspicuous. For the most part, he was treated equally by teachers and fellow students. A few teachers were mildly curious about his Afro-Asian appearance. Behind the closed doors of the teachers' lounge, some of the cantankerous veteran teachers and the curious newbie teachers dared to ask, "What's the deal with that kid?" Long time teachers recalled his older siblings (albeit adopted siblings) who fit the stereotypical American image. Given the reality of changing demographics and the superficial acceptance of diversity, these teachers' curiosity (and in some cases their contempt) was tamped down by political correctness. Times and sentiments were changing but old stereotypes die slowly.

Sammy got along well with his teachers. His siblings coached him well. Their advice was simply stay awake in class, show interest, and ask a question every so often. Northville's suburban school system was not considered academically rigorous so if you kept your eyes open and your mouth shut, you could get by. Sammy learned the basics but his real learning took place around the kitchen table, tagging along on mall patrols, and doing homework eavesdropping on mall cop briefings. Northville schools might be bland but they were a hell of a lot better than the chaotic classrooms of urban BellHaven.

One day in the playground as Sammy climbed to the top of the ladder for the slide, he decided to play king of the hill, foregoing his turn going down the slide. Two fair-haired, pony-tailed girls impatiently waited on the top rungs. Losing patience in the traffic jam, they shouted, "Move!"

Sammy, enjoying the view and his newfound power shouted back, "No!"

These short-tempered brats, used to getting their way, shouted back, "Stop being so Korean!" The slur was lost on Sammy whose interest shifted to sliding down head first. Maggie, hovering nearby with other moms, was stung by the comment. The suburban debutants couldn't care less. They were too busy discussing the trifles of online shopping to be cognizant of international atrocities. Maggie, on the other hand, was all too familiar with the devastation of Korea since Callahan would watch world news and documentaries on a 24/7 basis if he didn't have to work.

Sammy scampered to scale a nearby rock wall while Maggie tried to imagine what it would be like for him to grow up in a world minus Korea. No mom, no country, no ancestry. Well, at least he's got us, she thought with weary resignation. With eyes on Sammy, her dystopian mental chat continued. Thanks to the U.S. mantra "nuke 'em" we did just that to Korea. China and the U.S. cut a deal and swatted that pesky Korean mosquito. I can't believe I'm becoming a curmudgeon like Callahan. It's like Callahan always says, "Money talks, bullshit walks." Korea gambled. Called the U.S bluff. Sacrificed the whole peninsula, north and south. Came up on the short side of stubborn. And here I thought us Irish were the most stubborn people on Earth. Just shows how you got to pick your battles wisely.

Maggie's melancholy daydreaming was interrupted when Sammy fell off the rock wall. No permanent damage. Nothing an ice cream can't fix.

Family gatherings at Christmas, Easter, and birthdays included the standard interrogations of youngsters. "What's your favorite subject?"

Sammy's response, "Math and history," flustered them. They weren't accustomed to a binary response.

"Who's your favorite teacher?" was invariably their follow up question.

Without hesitation, Sammy selected, "Ms. Christina, my history teacher."

Ms. Christina had a petite frame and a feisty personality. Her brown eyes and coffee complexion mirrored Sammy's appearance. Beyond the physical similarities, Ms. Christina shared a cross-cultural connection. As a second generation Filipino American, she shared with Sammy an understanding of walking the tightrope of diversity and distrust. Higher-ups on the Board of Education appreciated her since she added diversity to the staff, which until recently had been lily white. Fellow teachers appreciated her fluency in Spanish and youthful exuberance. Her tough-love demeanor assisted with classroom and hallway management. Despite this appreciation, she confided in Sammy an uneasiness that, "Some days I feel like I'm nothing more than a placeholder, a photo op. Presenting an image for the powers that be."

As a typical teenager, Sammy clammed up when peppered by adult questions. Recollections of Ms. Christina loosened his tongue. "Diversity's a dual edged sword," said Sammy. "Some days I wonder if I'm liked because of who I am or if I'm being invited to parties so they feel better about themselves."

"You just be you and screw them if they got an attitude," was Callahan's standard response to this and most other touch and feely questions of an interpersonal nature.

"Being Afro-Asian, you're never sure if it's the Afro or the Asian background that's my entry ticket. I'm a mixed breed, I wonder what would have happened if the Afro dominated or vice versa," lamented Sammy who sought more guidance than the usual Trumanesque, "Give 'em hell," advice that Callahan routinely dispensed.

"Ms Christina told me how store clerks watched her like a hawk and I said, me too. Some teachers treat me like I'm a dummy and others expect me to be a brainiac. I told Ms.Christina and I'll tell you all, why don't they just let us be us?"

Overhearing Sammy's angst, Ralph assured him, "People just like thoroughbreds, that's why those blue bloods love the Westminster dog show. Don't they realize the smartest dogs are the mixed breeds?"

Butch was sitting nearby and the mention of Cristina's name and her Filipino background caught his attention. Looking up from the sports page, he asked, "What's Cristina's last name?"

"Ruiz," said Sammy.

Butch slapped his forehead exclaiming, "I can't believe she became a teacher. I remember when she used to run with a group of loud-mouthed girls. We used to toss them out of the mall every weekend. Hey, Ralph, remember that chick?"

Ralph shrugged, acknowledging that Butch was much better at remembering faces. Butch was still shaking his head saying, "How about that, now she's a teacher. Good for her. I guess some Puerto Ricans can turn out OK."

Sammy patiently reminded him that she was Filipino.

Ralph couldn't resist the opportunity to tell Butch, "We used to call you King Profiler. Now you're a frigging psychologist figuring out why people do stupid things. Now you're King of Second Chances."

"Don't throw me under that liberal bus," shot back Butch. "I got a long way to go before I become a snowflake giving everybody the benefit of the doubt."

Among the boys, Sammy's athleticism guaranteed he'd be the first picked for teams. Coaches already had him on their radar screens for what they hoped to be future championship seasons. Among the girls, Sammy's mixture of dark (but not black) skin, almond shaped eyes, and curly but not full Afro hair was intriguing in a subtle way.

As the years edged toward teenhood and early adulthood, his ability to smoothly navigate athletic and social circumstances would serve him well in all facets of life. His adopted brothers (Bryce, Kevin, and Bruce) gave him a heads up concerning what drama queens to avoid. They were the younger sisters of witches they tangled with, so he knew what poison ivy to avoid. Claire offered subtle insights about what girls like and don't like, since her brothers were clueless on such matters. Sammy frequently benefited from their expression, "If only I knew then what I know now."

Sammy's birth and childhood signaled an emotional watershed for all members of Callahan & Company. Everybody appreciated the need to step up to the plate. For his adopted siblings, they faced the usual challenges of finishing school and launching careers. There were documentaries to produce by Claire, mysteries of physics to unravel by Bryce, think tanks in need of thinkers like Kevin, and virtual reality games needing to be designed by Bruce. There was money to be made and connections to be forged. However, with Sammy coming up the ranks in their wake, the Callahan kids mentored Sammy while they were being mentored in their respective professions.

Young single guys on the mall cop force still lived with their parents. They had no other choice given the exorbitant housing costs coupled with low wages of mall cop salaries. They worked by day and partied by night. But when it was their turn to chip in, they contributed time and talents. Helping out Sammy made them realize, for the first time in their life, that they had skills worthy of sharing. Rookie Nicco interspersed his English with Spanish so Sammy mastered "Spanglish". When six-foot, eight-inch security officer Pierre ducked through the doorway of the Callahan household, he contributed a broad smile and a healthy sampling of Haitian dialect. Being dirt poor by USA standards, he visited empty handed but his booming voice and exuberant personality left everyone with the feeling that they had just visited Haiti (without the cost of airfare and minus personal safety issues). Nicco and Pierre were self-conscious of their linguistic mixed culture. In recent years, even the hint of an accent drew an angry stare from a good-old-boy just itching to un-conceal his Beretta at the slightest provocation. Sammy's exposure to mixed dialects as a child came in handy in dicey situations. Many a danger-ous alley was avoided and a fistfight averted thanks to Sammy's linguistic competencies and cultural empathy.

Looking back upon his childhood, Sammy com-mented, "I felt like I grew up in the United Nations."

Callahan proudly kept alive the Gaelic language and took pleasure in speaking Gaelic around others who didn't need to know what was being discussed. Callahan cautioned Sammy that, "It's becoming increasingly diffi-cult to discern friend from foe. Having a trusted inner circle of Gaelic speakers is an important vetting tech-nique."

Academically during the growing years, Sammy excelled not because he was a genius. In fact, on standardized tests, he scored in the average range during those early school years. Sammy had to study and do homework. Under the watchful eyes of the Callahans and extended family, he was frequently reminded to tend to his studies. What accelerated Sammy's progress in school was his exposure to experiential learning. While learning for other students was limited to reading about subjects, Sammy was experiencing the subjects. As the Mall Child, he hung out with the mall's cleaning crew, composed entirely of Spanish speakers. They adopted him in much the same way that mall cops took him under their wing. Over time, he was so conversant in Spanish that he could pass for a Latino, a characteristic that served him well in careers and travels. While fellow students crammed their brains with Spanish words that they promptly forgot after passing the test, Sammy internalized both the words and the culture.

The adage "the days are long but the years are short" applied to the Callahan household. There were science fairs to prepare for and book fairs to attend. The annual Diversity Dinner scheduled in the eighth grade triggered some interesting conversations in the Callahan household.

"I can cook up a storm, but soul food and Asian foods are not my thing," said Maggie.

"Maybe you could sponsor a potato table with mashed potatoes and baked potatoes like they display apple pies and blueberry pies," offered Callahan in a lame attempt to be helpful.

"And you could dress up as Mr. Potato Head," shot back Maggie. "I'm gonna stick with what I know. I'll donate a shepherd's pie with Irish soda bread on the side."

"Make extra to bring home," added Sammy who was working on his homework in a corner of the kitchen. In other families, kids were squirreled away in their bedrooms on the premise that they were doing homework when they actually were mindlessly scrolling social media. The oversized Callahan kitchen was reminiscent of the colonial hearth where all eating and conversing took place and secrets were harder to keep.

Glancing away from a documentary on the History Channel explaining how the race riots of the 1960s are being redefined as uprisings rather than mere riots, Callahan said, "This ethnic dinner stuff reminds me we're going down to New York City next month for the annual St. Patrick's Day parade. Hey, Sammy, do you still have that big button that says 'Kiss Me I'm Irish'?"

"It's still in my drawer where it belongs," said Sammy, thinking of the absurdity of an Afro-Asian kid wearing this obnoxious button. He pretended to be reading a boring story about a guy who got swallowed up by a whale while it was getting under his nerves about how some teachers seemed to call him out whenever diversity events were scheduled. Why can't I be Sammy from nowhere? Some days I just want to hide. Other days I wish I knew more about my Korean roots, thought Sammy as he pretended to be reading.

Before they knew it, St. Patty's Day arrived. On the train ride back from a day of screeching bagpipes, Sammy asked Maggie about his Korean roots. "There's plenty of African American history. We're in the arts, politics and sports. You got Martin Luther King Jr., Booker T. Washington, Michael Jordan, Michael Jackson, and on and on. So where's the Korean movers and shakers?"

Maggie was at a loss for words. "Let's check the internet when we get back," said Maggie who was one of the last Americans whose iPhone was not surgically attached to her hip. Once home, her search revealed that Psy of the "Gangnam Style" song topped the list of Korean notables. Maggie was no fan of rappers and she sighed with exasperation, "There must be more to Korean history and culture than this! Sorry Psy, no harm intended."

Summer school recess was only a few months away, so it was decided that another trip to NYC be scheduled to check out the Korean Museum of History and Culture. The trip included a visit to the Korean Way (a.k.a., West 32nd Street in mid-Manhattan), not far from the Empire State Building. Sammy was old enough to observe that every city seemed to have a Martin Luther King Street but there was only one place called Korean Way. Upon entry to the museum, there was the usual chronology of people, places, and events.

Like so many ancient cultures, Korea had a long history of kings and dynasties. Most prominent among the kings was Sejong the Great. Sammy quipped, "You can't go wrong researching someone with the title 'The Great'. Sejong the Great certainly earned that title. He was responsible for developing the Korean alphabet and keeping Chinese and Japanese invaders at bay. In Korean history, fending off incursions by the Chinese and Japanese was important for keeping the peninsula Korean.

The only recorded downside of Sejong the Great was some intolerance of Muslims."

Maggie exclaimed, "That sounds familiar, what's that saying, the more things change, the more they stay the same?" When Maggie was reading the detailed history of Sejong the Great, she lingered on the paragraph concerning his battle with diabetes. It described how he was able to defeat the Chinese and Japanese pirates but he ultimately went blind and died of diabetes. Sammy had to snap Maggie from her trance to remind her that the museum was about to close. She was famous for losing track of time. On the journey back home, Sammy had to read to Maggie the directional signals at Grand Central Station so they could board the right train. On the return trip, she was not her chatty self and it was apparent that the field trip had taken its toll.

Chapter 8:
Father's Day

Callahan received a call from Bryce wishing him a Happy Father's Day.

"What type of mad scientist stuff are you cooking up?"

"Nothing I can talk about, top secret."

"Just make sure you get patents. Don't give away your thoughts. I did that for thirty years and see where it got me."

"I won't," said Bryce, going no further for fear of falling down a Callahan rabbit hole rant.

"Guess what I saw on my shift yesterday?" Callahan asked.

"What?" said Bryce with everyone else listening on the speaker phone in Callahan's kitchen.

"I stumbled upon a child being conceived in a car along the back wall of the parking garage."

"How romantic," said an exasperated Maggie who heard countless such stories.

"How sad. Another mouth to feed. Roosters don't stick around for parenting. Junior's a good example. He had a rooster dad and a daffy duck mom," quipped

Butch. "No wonder his head is full of conspiracies and fantasies."

As soon as he voiced disdain for roosters, he glanced toward Sammy who was preoccupied with dishwashing.

Silence hung in the air like the interval between the clap of thunder and flash of lightning.

"I finished homework. OK to play naval *Call of Duty*?" asked Sammy who was already heading down the hallway toward his bedroom.

"Sure," said Maggie, the air traffic controller when it came to assigning tasks.

"Too many kids grow up wondering who's my daddy?," commented Butch. "If Sammy has these thoughts, he doesn't express them."

"I only tell him what I know about his mother, and that's not much. Maybe she's somewhere in the States. She's not in Korea, that's for sure," said Maggie.

"The USA put the screws to Korea. Squashed it like a bug," chimed in Bryce who reminded everyone he was still on speaker phone.

"As for Sammy's father, how much can you say about a sperm deposit?" said Maggie with the finality of a judge pounding a gavel.

"Who needs a father when you have Callahan and us. He must know we've got his back," said Butch, recovering from his rooster comment. "Unlike Junior, we kept him inside the guardrails."

"We know he's loved. I think he knows he's loved. Let's not start throwing around that four letter word in this Irish American household," said Callahan.

"Speaking of love, I forgot to mention the bumper sticker I saw on the car next to those love birds," continued Callahan.

"Did it say something like 'Virginia is for lovers' or 'South of the border'?" asked Butch.

"No, it said, 'Help America, Pray the Rosary, Pro-Life'," said Callahan.

"You know," said Butch, leaning forward as if to share some deep, dark family secret, "Sammy wouldn't have been here if she made another decision."

"That worked out good for Sammy. I wish every kid had us," said Callahan. "Here's what else I wish …

"I wish the roosters kept it in their pants or at least stepped up to the plate.

"I wish the holy rollers stepped up to the plate.

"I wish society stepped up to the plate.

"There wouldn't be such a shit show if everybody pulled their weight."

As Butch aimlessly stirred his soup, which was now getting cold, all he could add was, "If only they did, if only that was true."

Chapter 9:
Absurdities, Antics, and Adaptations

For Callahan and the mall cop crew, the slightest act of absurdity triggered an avalanche of exaggerations. Rookie mall cop Nicco was zooming around on his patrol bike rounding up Target carts. His nickname was the energizer bunny. Out of breath, he yelled to Callahan who pulled up in the mall's pickup truck, "Maybe we could have a rickshaw to pull around an aging mall cop."

"Very funny," scoffed Callahan.

Undeterred, Nicco continued, "Shoppers could be peddled around in carriages like those horse-drawn carriages in Central Park in New York City."

"Sure, why not," humored Callahan. "The mall cops could be issued racing go-karts like the Shriners buzzing in circles at parades. People would come from far and wide to see mall cops in go-karts, mini-bikes and rickshaws."

"We got to do something or else they'll board up this place and we'll be out of a job," said Nicco.

"You know who this mall needs to turn it around?" said Callahan.

"Who's that?" asked Nicco.

"We need a guy named P.T. Barnum. He's the ultimate showman. Created the *Greatest Show on Earth*. Lived right here in BellHaven."

"So let's get him," said Nicco with youthful exuberance. "We could have six-foot, eight-inch guard Pierre chasing around five foot, two inch guard Leslie on roller skates. Making this a three-ring circus."

"Getting P.T. Barnum here might be a problem," sighed Callahan. "He's been dead for years and so has BellHaven, for that matter."

Nicco was one of the few rookie mall cops with the ingredients for a career in law enforcement. Most other rookies viewed the job as a gig filling the time gap between general studies classes at the community college while pursuing nebulous career goals. For others, working was that portion of the day that serves only as an interruption from their steady diet of gaming and social media trawling. Not so for Nicco. His Hawaiian roots on his mom's side blessed him with a bulky physique. Ideal for emerging from a patrol car and requesting to see licenses and registration at traffic stops. Puerto Rican lineage on his dad's side imbued him with the feistiness of a Chihuahua. This came in handy when situations got hot. However, Callahan's ability to tamp down his own Irish temper mentored Nicco and averted visits to the human resources office.

Wacky ideas and a bevy of other absurdities were bantered about at Burpees lunch counter and at the bar at Willy's Water Hole. With shopping at malls on the decline due to online shopping and an ever-growing sense of insecurity on the streets, Callahan & Company approached mall management with their ideas about experiential events.

Much to their surprise, their suggestions were supported by mall management who were desperate for tactics to increase foot traffic. Over time and with some practice (and bumps and bruises) the mall cop force took on a Cirque Du Soleil quality. Their fleet included mopeds, tricycles, and even a vehicle that resembled the Batmobile. Some mall cops dressed as superhero characters while others donned cartoon character outfits. The mall appealed to persons of all ages and fans of various genres. Costumes and skits ranged from *Star Wars* to Marvel comics to the Cartoon Network.

The role model for this endeavor was Disney World where patrons rarely (if ever) see intimidating uniformed security presence. Visitors see plenty of animated characters performing double duty as both entertainers and security.

This new strategy proved highly successful since patrons came from near and far to be entertained by mall cop antics. The strategy further cemented camaraderie among mall cops, similar to the bonding that occurs among a theater troupe performing on a daily basis. The mall cops of Renaissance Center became legendary. The mall was transitioning from a shopping destination to an experiential marketplace where you could see things and be seen. The mall cop force continued to recruit wannabe cops since they still served a prevent, respond, and report function. However, aspiring actors, entertainers, and comedians were now also joining the force to build

up their résumés. Times had changed and Callahan &
Company were changing with the times.

Callanan and Peter Pan could have been cousins. He
might look old but he never grew up. He liked to say,
"Why grow up? Why be normal?"

Antics provide a temporary relief from the daily
stream of bombings, beheadings, and mayhem in the
post-9/11 world of endless war against elusive enemies.

Callahan frequently lectured to anyone of the Callahan & Company crew who would listen that, "Antics
create a bond among persons who otherwise have no
reason to bond. The antidote to isolation is a shared absurdity."

As a Saturday night shift drew to a close, Callahan
spotted the giant bunny head stashed in storage since the
next day was Easter Sunday. The costume would no
longer be needed since the mall would be closed. Shift
change is prime time for antics. Escapades concocted by
the evening shift terrorized the midnight shift. Callahan
donned the giant bunny head and instructed Wendy the
dispatcher to direct MadMan Jermaine to check on the
truck tunnel on the premise that a midnight skateboarder
was reportedly caught on camera in the vicinity. As luck
would have it, the massive metal door to the truck tunnel
was broken and only a chain stretched across the open-
ing, hardly a deterrent to a mischievous skateboarder. To
add plausibility to the story, Sammy gladly played the role
of skateboarder, luring MadMan Jermaine into the truck
tunnel.

There was a good reason that Jermaine was nicknamed MadMan. He grew up in "The Village" in

BellHaven. He was a product of mean streets. He fondly described a childhood experience when he and a young cousin were treated to ice cream. So far so good but the crazy uncle who provided the treat said he had to make a stop before they indulged in that refreshment on a hot summer night. Jermaine and his cousin waited anxiously in the car until they heard a blast from a nearby porch. Crazy uncle hopped in the driver's seat and they sped off to the ice cream shop where he made good on his promise. He was a man of his word and he made good on his promises, just like he made good on the promise to knee-cap the gentleman on the porch who was screwing around with his old lady. Jermain grew up to be six-foot, four-inches and developed his own style of martial arts forged from a few formal lessons and plenty of street brawls.

Upon his entry into the truck tunnel, Callahan in his enormous bunny head emerged from the shadows bellowing, "Happy Easter!" MadMan Jermaine instinctively assumed a Karate stance, about to pounce on bunny's head. Callahan shouted, "It's Callahan," and Jermaine relaxed his posture. Annihilation averted. Sammy had great fun helping pull off this skit and many other successful antics. Over time, a repertoire of antics built up and were retold at Willy's Water Hole and Burpees Diner, just like stories shared by cowboys around the campfire in the Old West. Accumulate enough stories and you form a foundation of camaraderie that unites even the most diverse and divisive batch of people. There's an old saying, you're remembered not by what you said and not by what you did. You're remembered by how you made them feel. For Callahan & Company, communal craziness was that feeling.

Callahan bolstered the spirits of members of Callahan & Company, reminding them that antics and escapades in life are what we most fondly recall. He frequently reminded them, "They're the tales that get told and retold and sometimes evolve into legends. The deeper the reservoir of stories, antics, and episodes, the richer the relationships and the richer the life." Callahan, his relatives, and the extended family of Callahan & Company drew strength and support from this rich reservoir of antics. Sammy had a front and center seat to this foolishness and he came to appreciate its value many years later.

Chapter 10:
Canaries in the Mine

The years drifted by and times got easier depending upon your keyboarding and surfing skills. For Callahan, his keyboarding was limited by carpal tunnel. His surfing was limited to lap swimming. His son Bruce took to computers like a fish to water. He had fun with Callahan who struggled with all things technical. No incident better illustrated the technology gap than the time Bruce and his siblings were reviewing the Facebook page of a long-lost relative.

Callahan peered over their shoulder and exclaimed, "Wow, she gained some weight!"

To this Bruce quipped, "Shh, she can hear you over Facebook." Callahan was momentarily ashamed of his verbal observation until they all burst out laughing, assuring him that Facebook had not gotten that sophisticated, at least not yet. The Callahan kids and Sammy patiently imparted tech tips to Callahan in moderate doses so he was not overwhelmed. Callahan muddled along but deep down he knew he was a dinosaur coasting along in the last quarter of this technology game.

This Facebook exchange sparked Callahan to launch into one of his many tirades about how technology was making everything more complicated. His primary target was the default expressions "there's an app for that" and "go to the website." He loved to recall the story of how a coworker at one of his office jobs was concerned about the weather for his ride home but was having trouble pulling up the weather app. Callahan assured him that a storm was imminent based on the gathering of gray clouds and the upturned leaves on trees in the swirling wind as viewed from the office window.

Callahan was not the only canary in the mine concerning tech advances. The mine itself had become a canary. Retail had shifted to online purchases and home delivery was raising questions about the viability of malls. The security industry was shifting from labor intensive touring of sites to drones canvassing sites from above with cameras. Smart cards were monitoring and controlling access from central locations.

Class warfare had also created a level of tension that necessitated home-schooling, home-shopping, and what came to be known as protective nesting. Leisurely shopping, strolling, and venturing outdoors became things of the past. Kids no longer roamed freely and segments of society had become so polarized that discussing anything more significant than the weather or sports might trigger rage. Callahan observed that signs posted at businesses used to simply announce "No Soliciting." Now they specified:

- No Religion
- No Politics
- No Canvassing

- No Free Samples

Callahan exclaimed in his increasingly cranky and quirky moments that, "Soon they'll be no opinions, no questioning, no thinking."

Road rage was no longer limited to the road. Now rage was the norm in all its ugly forms.

Protective nesting was the defensive response to this state of affairs. Insulating family and friends from "the others" became a survival tactic. Avoidance of OTHERS included those whose views and backgrounds differed from you and threatened you, your family, and friends. Beyond the threat posed by the ideological and philosophical differences with OTHERS, there was a growing sense of physical intimidation from OTHERS. Lively discussions at the Callahan dinner table with Book TV or a historic documentary playing in the background always circled back to the state of world affairs and the arc of history.

Ever the history buff, Callahan explained, "There always existed a fear of being caught on the 'other side of the tracks' or on the 'wrong side of town'. Even ancient Rome and Athens had their bad neighborhoods."

Callahan's "kitchen cabinet" as he liked to refer to them, consisted of an ever-changing mixture of whomever happened to visit between work and school schedules. One thing they all agreed upon was the sense of fear that crept into everyone's psyche. Where strangers gathered, no matter how benign they may appear, there was a growing sense that they could not be trusted. Tribalism was on the rise as a defense mechanism to this growing sense of social isolation.

Callahan & Company adapted and survived in this environment because they were by definition both inclusive and exclusive. They were inclusive because they were an eclectic and eccentric mix of characters. They were exclusive because of their all for one, one for all and watch-your-back approach to life.

Chapter 11:
The Good, the Odd, the Bad, and the Ugly

Sammy palled around with mall cops during his growing years. He was the mall mascot the way a Dalmatian is adopted by a fire house. It was during his gap year (after high school but before military service) that he got a full taste of human nature … the good, the odd, the bad, and the ugly.

<u>The Good</u>

The good includes little moments of life with positive connectivity among humans. They're not spectacular interactions but collectively they offer a ray of hope for the future. As a youngster, Sammy heard enough of these stories to give credence to the belief that the glass of humanity is half full. When he was old enough to tag along on "mall calls" and blend in on the premise that he was "in training", he got to see qualities of goodness and kindness first hand.

There was the time a teen girl was frantic at mall closing because she left her pink purse in the customer lounge. There it was, safe and sound, perched on the couch with valuables intact. Lounging next to it were teens who by all outward appearances were troublemakers. Lesson learned: looks can be deceiving and pre-judgment should be avoided.

There was the time an elderly white woman was found on the ground by a passerby in the parking lot. A Latino mom and her teen daughter comforted her till security arrived. It turned out that the woman was suffering aftereffects of the morning's chemo treatments. Despite her illness and loss of hair, her sense of humor remained intact. When asked about her identity (standard procedure for report writing), she said, "I'm Joan," and added with a wry smile, "I'm wanted in all fifty states."

When Callahan checked her ID, he observed that her address matched one of BellHaven's toughest neighborhoods. Callahan knew BellHaven like the back of his hand having been a community organizer many years earlier. He thought to himself, A person's age and where they reside can explain much about them. It lends insight to what motivates them. Why do they think and act the way they do? It can explain what makes them tick.

Callahan observed that Joan's date of birth made her five years younger than him. Her illness and a life of hard times easily added ten years to her appearance. Joan declined an ambulance and said she would take the bus home. Upon hearing this and knowing how tough Joan's neighborhood was, the Latino mom offered to drive her home. She provided positive modeling for her teen daughter. Sammy witnessed compassion in action. Since it was a few weeks before Christmas, Sammy commented, "This must be the true spirit of Christmas."

As the radio in the mall patrol vehicle cranked out another report of an act of police brutality, Callahan commented, "This is like Groundhog Day, another white cop shooting a black kid after a traffic stop. I'm not a big technology guy, but can't we figure out a way to stop police chases?"

"*Na biodh imni ort*," Sammy responded to Callahan. That's Gaelic for "don't worry about it". During ride alongs, Sammy and Callahan liked to brush up on Gaelic.

Sammy continued, "I love the expressions on shoppers when they see a guy like me speaking in a language that they can't identify. Back to your technology idea, let's put kill switches in all vehicles so cops can stop the criminal. Better yet, let's plant chips in criminals' asses to keep track of them."

To this Callahan asked Sammy, "You know what really scares me? You're starting to talk like me. I'm usually the negative one with the crazy ideas. Now how about some more positive stories?"

"Sure," said Sammy.

"OK," said Callahan as he perused through his battered notepad that records incidents. "Remember the time cops responded to a teenage girl having an epileptic seizure in the foyer of Macys? Cops break up fights and slap on handcuffs, so seeing them treat this distressed girl with care and respect was noteworthy. They also comforted the girl's friend who was freaking out."

"Most cops are OK but you know some can be dicks," said Sammy, who had been well trained by Callahan to keep his head down and his mouth shut when traveling in towns where the cops didn't know him.

"You got some bad apples out there. In some defense of them, I got to tell you about the time they responded to a call concerning a mentally deranged black male wandering in the parking lot. I was first on scene. I approached this spiky haired guy with green cargo pants and a Bob Marley T-shirt. He was standing on top of one of those stone monuments, the ones installed to prevent a truck from crashing into the entrance. From this perch, he was posing like he was shooting an arrow to the stars."

"What did he say? What did you do?" asked Sammy.

"When I asked him, hey buddy what's up? Mr. Arrow Shooter leaped down. Scared the shit out of me but I didn't show it. He still didn't say anything."

"Then what happened?" asked Sammy.

"Well, he took up residence by a vehicle in the middle of the parking lot. The two responding cops questioned him from a safe distance in a defensive stance as standard protocol. I noticed they treated him as a valued human being. Turns out that the vehicle he was standing next to belonged to the family that brought him to the mall. All's well, ends well."

"Too bad every call doesn't end well," commented Sammy.

As Callahan finished his coffee, he let Sammy know that in a different time and at a different place, the outcome might have been much different for a deranged black male confronting two white cops.

"Maybe not all that different," countered Sammy.

"We're making progress but nothing changes overnight. In the meantime, be patient and for God's sake be cool if you get pulled over," cautioned Callahan.

"Hey, every car has a sun visor, right?" asked Sammy.

"Sure, what's that got to do with anything?"

"Well if every sun visor had a pouch where the license and registration could be pulled when the cops demand, 'License and registration, please,' black guys would not have to reach over to the glove compartment or reach into their back pocket. Might save a few from getting killed."

"Sounds like a reasonable solution. Practical and low cost. Why don't you propose that when you run for office?"

"I just might do that."

"Hey, remember Rosa who misplaced her car?" asked Callahan.

"Somebody loses their car almost every shift. How am I supposed to remember Rosa?"

"That one I remember and I'll tell you why. She was an elderly African American woman who was a retired teacher. She proudly noted she was the first in her family to go to college. First black teacher hired in BellHaven."

"None of this stuff has anything to do with finding her car. So why the history lesson about Rosa?" asked Sammy who occasionally got impatient when conversations did not sprint to the bottom line.

"Because riding around looking for somebody's car is when you get a snapshot into the life of a stranger. It actually makes this job interesting," responded Callahan who had reunited many people with their vehicle.

"I see what you mean. A few sentences with someone and you get a sense of where they've been, what they've done and what they're all about," agreed Sammy.

"I remember asking Rosa what subject she taught. She said accounting. That's when I told her I flunked that twice. I sensed she had a distinguished teaching career and would have been a favorite teacher even in a subject as dry as accounting. Rosa said that by explaining cost/benefit analysis to inner-city kids in terms of buying sneakers, the subject came alive for them. She said she instilled in some of them the importance of saving and for this she was both proud and grateful."

"Wish I had a teacher like her. I'm not good with numbers either," said Sammy.

"Anyways," continued Callahan, "we looked everywhere for that vintage, dark green Ford Crown Victoria. Rosa mentioned that it was her late husband's car and it was still in mint condition. I sensed that her marriage had also been in mint condition."

Sammy was gazing absentmindedly across the vast parking lot extending out to the bus shelter, seemingly uninterested but Callahan's observations were soaking in like water on a sponge.

"You know, Sammy, if you meet enough people and read between the lines, you can gain insight concerning their backstory. Rosa said she enjoyed driving her Crown Vic in the left lane, the fast lane of the Parkway, since motorists thought she was a cop. They all pulled over to the right lane. Everybody's entitled to their guilty pleasures and Rosa was entitled to hers. Upon finding her Crown Vic, remember how she unlocked the door but waved for further assistance?"

"I remember her now," said Sammy. "She was a cool old person. It was freezing and we figured she needed a jumpstart. Instead, she gave you $6 with instructions to get yourself a beer."

"You know who she reminded me of?" asked Callahan.

"Who?" said Sammy.

"Rosa Parks, same first name, same story. Just a local version with less publicity."

"I got another story. This happened before your time riding around with me. Did I ever tell you about 'Door Four Joe'?"

"No, what was the deal with him?"

"Well, that wasn't his real name but door number four was his spot. He was sharply dressed in a tie and jacket topped off with a fedora hat. He stood guard at door number four most afternoons. He dutifully waited for his granddaughter to end her shift at Build-A-Bear. Being a grandfatherly escort was his official reason for standing guard. His ulterior motive was to socialize and see the world go by."

Another story about some cool old person, thought Sammy, but he kept this thought to himself having learned to not interrupt Callahan on one of his voyages into the past.

"In his day," continued Callahan, "Door Four Joe saw a lot of the world and it wasn't all pretty. He was in the square in Italy when they hung Mussolini from a lamppost as World War II was winding down. He escaped to America to pursue the American dream, which became a reality for him after years of hard labor as a bricklayer. This explained his firm handshake at age ninety-two and why he was such a dapper dresser. After years of wearing dusty overalls, dressing sharp was a symbol of success. His odyssey also explained why he so strongly supported immigrants in the face of recent animosity toward them."

"Wow, I've read about that stuff. You met the real deal."

"Well you know how I'm a practical joker?" said Callahan.

"You're the king of practical jokers. That's why everybody hides from you on April Fools' Day," quipped Sammy.

"Well, this was one of my best practical jokes. I observed Door Four Joe sleeping soundly in an overstuffed chair. His chest was barely moving, his head tilted back on a pillow, his mouth wide open, and drooling a little bit. Hardly the image of his usual dignified self. I couldn't resist announcing as rookie guard Nicco rounded the corner that he was posted at this site waiting for the coroner. 'The coroner!' said Nicco. Yea, poor old Door Four Joe died," I told him. "Very sad, we'll all certainly miss him."

"Poor Nicco. He's such a straight arrow. Roger-dodger's his middle name, hangs on your every word," said Sammy.

"Well, he was clearly flustered and reached for his radio to report this to dispatch but stopped short since he wasn't sure what code to transmit. I finally broke the tension reassuring him that Door Four Joe was fine and was just catching up on some zees.

"That's not the end of the story," said Callahan.

"There's more?" said Sammy.

"Yea, a few weeks later, Door Four Joe really did die. He succumbed to cancer which he kept to himself to the very end. A contingent of guards attended his wake held at the nearby funeral parlor. You know, Sammy, Door Four Joe's stories of triumph over tyranny in Italy and success in America gives us much-needed inspiration as another member of the Greatest Generation faded into the annals of history. Bet they didn't teach you that in history class?"

"They teach some of this but it's not like anybody's listening."

"Well, they better listen up before it's too late," admonished Callahan.

The Odd

This group requires its own category. They're not necessarily good or bad or ugly. They are simply odd. They're quirky. They're people that become the human landscape that uniquely defines each locality. They're the people you don't notice if you're just passing through. But spend any extended time in any one place and you can't help but notice them. Once you accept them as part of the local scene and as long as there's nothing overtly threatening about them, their presence actually provides a sense of security. In an odd way, they ground us. They offer a sense that we're "home". They're the human wallpaper, the backdrop of our busy lives.

Back in the Callahan kitchen, Callahan asked Sammy, "How's the essay coming along? You have to submit that application to the Coast Guard Academy pretty soon, right?"

"I'm sort of stuck. Why can't I just apply, go, and get trained? What's with all the heavy duty questions they put on the application?"

"They want to know you can do more than drive a boat and shoot a gun.

"I got an idea, how about writing about the odd birds you've met hanging around the mall? There's plenty of material there. Your essay could ask the following questions: How did they get here? Who are they?"

"All good questions but how do I write an essay around them?" asked Sammy between spoonfuls of ice cream, which always enhances writing abilities.

"Go deep, get beneath the surface. Admissions counselors love that stuff. Ask questions like, what was their life like, where do they go, and what makes them return like homing pigeons?" said Callahan.

"Who are we talking about?" asked Sammy. "So many oddballs, you're gonna have to cut the list."

"Don't worry. Pick any. People love to hear true stories about real people," said Callahan.

Sammy gazed into space, trying his best to stay awake and focus on Callahan's long-winded advice.

"You should describe Rasputin. Long beard, dreadlocks, sunglasses at night, layers of clothing, and plenty of shopping bags," continued Callahan..

"I just thought he was a homeless, dangerous guy."

"No, the real story is he lives in a nearby house that he inherited from parents. He's actually kind of effeminate and timid."

"Is that why you shut off the overhead flashers on the truck when you approach him?"

"Yea, bright flashing lights bother him."

"I remember the time you got out of the vehicle to head him off from re-entering the mall at closing time and a soccer mom with her tweens pulled them close thinking he was gonna flip out," nodded Sammy.

"I'm no psychologist," said Callahan, "but Rasputin exhibits passive/aggressive behaviors. When told the mall is closed, he sneaks around to other entrances so he can rummage for more cans to redeem."

"So Rasputin's a good example of how looks are deceiving. We need to find out the real deal about somebody," said Sammy.

"Exactly," said Callahan.

"I got one for you," said Uncle Ralph. "What about the odd couple? Not the Felix & Oscar neat nick/slob duo we used to watch on TV. Sorry Sammy, this was way before your time. Only Callahan and I probably remember them."

"I do remember the mall's odd couple," said Sammy. "They were a middle-aged male and female team. It wasn't clear if they were husband and wife or brother and sister. I always assumed it was the latter."

"They were an affable couple, quick to offer a smile and wave," said Callahan. "Seems like they belong to that cadre of people who brighten our lives with light conversations about the weather but not much else."

"Yea, they seemed inseparable but after a while, the female was AWOL. Where the hell did she go?" asked Ralph. "I asked him one day, where's your friend? And you know what he said?"

"What?" asked Sammy who recalled seeing them but didn't think much more about them.

"He just said, 'Not here.' It gave me the creeps. But I followed the universal male rule of 'don't pry' and 'leave it alone'."

"Rumor has it," said Callahan with a mischievous smile, "that she's buried in his backyard along with several other bodies. To this day, he still walks the mall waving to one and all. Keep it light and keep it moving, that's the mall cop mantra," said Callahan.

"All this time and we still don't know their names. Sounds like they're the wallpaper of our lives," said Sammy.

"Write that down, that's the jargon you got to put in the college essay. They love that stuff," said Callahan who back in the day had written his share of college essays and grant applications.

"Speaking of characters with names, how about Lucas?" said Ralph. "Potbellied, suspender-wearing guy with a wild mop of black hair roaming the mall singing and talking to himself. He had good and bad days depending upon his medication dosage."

"How could I forget Lucas?" said Callahan. "One day I was having a casual conversation with him on a Sunday afternoon in the food court, I asked him who's your favorite band? Lucas answered, 'U2.' I said it was one of my favorites not just because they're from Ireland but also because I like their lyrics.

"Then I made the mistake of asking, what's your favorite U2 song? Lucas responded, 'Sunday Bloody Sunday,' which he belted out at the top of his lungs amid the food court crowd. Patrons scurried in all directions and I had to coax him to lower the decibel."

"Lucas could be a one-man riot," added Butch.

"Speaking of riots, you got to hear this," continued Callahan. "There I was, pumping gas at midnight at the gas station down the street next to Willy's Water Hole. This particular night was ladies' night and there were scantily clad women in their twenties partying on the sidewalk in the overflow bar crowd. Couples were arguing, guys with beer muscles were fighting. College kids were vomiting and cops were on the way. It was a classic donnybrook."

"Sounds like my kind of night out, why didn't you call me to join you?" laughed Butch.

"Well, lo and behold, there was Lucas in the middle of this mess," continued Callahan. "He was surrounded by hot-looking chicks. His eyes were bugged out, his mouth wide open and only one of his suspenders was holding up his pants. The expression on his face shouted out, I must have died and gone to heaven!"

"I hope his zipper was up," said Ralph.

"I didn't get close enough to check that," admonished Callahan.

"What was he doing down there at that hour?" asked Sammy.

"He lived above the bar and the commotion must have woken him up. Next day when he saw me at the mall, he told me, 'You wouldn't believe the dream I had last night'."

"Hey, you know who we haven't seen in a while?" asked Sammy who was jotting down his list of characters to weave into his application essay. "Who remembers the Dancing Egyptian?"

"Oh yea, he was a swarthy, pudgy, middle-aged dude clad entirely in white. Neatly pressed, starched white pants, white shirt, socks, and sneakers. He usually stationed himself by the concierge desk," recalled Ralph. "I also remember he wore beats (white, of course) and danced to the beat of his beats."

"You know who he reminded me of?" said Callahan.

"Who?" said Sammy.

"Picture Inspector Clouseau of the *Pink Panther* series dancing to rap music. That was the Dancing Egyptian. His dance tour lasted about one year and then he went to parts unknown. Like so many characters in this menagerie, we don't know what brought them here and we don't know where they go. But while passing through, they certainly are entertaining," said Callahan.

"So what does the future hold for these oddballs?" asked Sammy.

"Who knows," mused Callahan, "and for that matter, what does the future hold for us?"

As each year drew to a close, lively conversations around the Callahan kitchen table included recounting of odd birds who nested at the mall. This annual review of characters mirrored the year end magazine review of society's movers and shakers and remembrance of those who passed away. The ebb and flow of mall characters brought color to the monotonous canvas of mall cops plodding around the common areas and riding in circles patrolling its parking lots.

Sammy was finishing up washing dishes, and twins Claire and Kevin were putting dishes away while Bryce was vacuuming the living room. Bruce got a pass on chores this evening since he promised to de-bug a friend's computer. He couldn't turn down some cash from a side job. Everybody in Callahan's world had to pull their own weight and raise cash wherever it could be found. Maggie was already fast asleep on the couch in the family room with the TV blaring a useless infomercial once her favorite episode of *Downton Abbey* ended. Conversations wound down as members of the kitchen cabinet tended to chores and drifted off. There were phone calls to make and movies to watch.

With no one left in the kitchen, Callahan licked clean his plate of beef stroganoff and polished off his Narragansett beer. He turned off the kitchen light, leaving only the bluish glow of the nightlight over the sink. In the solitude of kitchen shadows, he mumbled to himself, "I wonder if they'll remember me when I'm gone. Will they wonder where I've migrated to? For that matter, where am I headed when this ridiculous treadmill of life stops? Oh well, too late and too tired to start thinking about that heavy shit," and with that he shuffled off to bed for a long winter's nap.

The Bad

To the casual observer, they are cute and hold promise for the future. They wear nice clothes and under different circumstances, they could have been honor students. But they sit in the lock-up room of loss prevention departments. Once they open their mouths, their shallowness shines through. Most often they steal because they can. It's just what they do. They're not starving or homeless but they are morally bankrupt. Every other word out of their crass little mouths is "fuck you". Their world revolves around them. Where will they be in ten years? One can only hope for the best but pragmatically speaking they will keep stealing and bear children and not much else.

Their male shoplifting counterparts are no different. No better. Handsome, well dressed, and well fed, it begs the question, why do they steal? More troubling is the question, why are they so angry? They spit, swear, and glare. Both guys and gals who steal hoot and holler before they are detained. They mumble when interrogated and claim to carry no identification. Once the police arrive they discover both their voice and their ID.

Their mugshots line the walls of the mall cops' lunchroom, providing endless banter.

Butch and Ralph held the record for memorizing faces of banned persons. "Snagging these repeat trespassers is like fishin' in a barrel," exclaimed Butch.

"Sometimes I spot them but I gotta play it cool since I play ball with some of them," said Nicco.

As Callahan munched on his ham and cheese sandwich, he said, "I give up, how can I recognize these mutts when I'm only here on weekends. Plus they keep changing hair styles and dying their hair. You know what really bothers me about these mugshots?"

"What's that?" said Sammy who had a sixth sense about Callahan going into a deeper tunnel of thought rather than a shallow trench of conversation.

"Each mug shot could have been a baby picture. We all think kids are cute when they're young. The sky's the limit. They're all gonna be presidents. Next thing you know, we got our hand on the taser when they reach inside their jacket."

"So when do they go sour, like a peach left out too long in the sun?" said Butch as he spit out the pit of his own over ripened peach.

"I'll tell you when they go south. It's in middle school, at the boy-meets-girl stage," said Nicco who was not all that many years removed from the middle school world.

"I say it's no father, no role model," said Ralph. "If I had kids, I would have been a role model."

"We deal with them in short bursts, can you imagine being a teacher and dealing with these assholes day in and day out?" sighed Callahan.

"No thanks," said Butch and Ralph in unison.

"I wonder if maybe we should give up on big schools that just warehouse these kids. Maybe we could have micro-schooling. How about home-schooling on steroids where they get intensively mentored and coached. Maybe they could spend half the day being taught and the other half of the day job shadowing. I worked for years in public housing and you know what kids ask for?" said Callahan.

"Who's my real father?" shot back Ralph who frequently forgot that Sammy was present.

"They ask for cash. They want purpose. They want to learn, even though they never admit that," said Callahan.

Sammy thought to himself, Just another of Callahan's idea dumps.

"So who's gonna pay for all this micro-teaching, mentoring bullshit," asked Butch.

Before Callahan could respond, Ralph gave his usual response, "USA taxpayers pay."

Undeterred, Callahan suggested, "Micro-teaching and mentoring might shorten the time these kids are in school. It might in the long run actually save money."

As with most lunchroom conversations, nothing got settled but the seed of thought was planted. Sammy absorbed the dialogue like a sponge absorbs water to be drained out at a later date.

The Ugly

Persons who merit the ugly category are those whose criminal behavior or demonstrated hate for humanity bump them up from the bad category. They are the armed robbers of a jewelry store. Ugly includes a shoplifter who ran from Lord & Taylor and had to be tackled by Corporal Wheeler and the store detective with an assist by Callahan.

What made the capture more dangerous than the usual grab and run was the fact that the suspect's biceps were as large as his captors' thighs. As if that was not enough, he carried a brass knuckle that was fashioned into a switchblade knife. A beautiful silver-plated ornament, had it not been for its deadly potential. The suspect had so many aliases that it was past midnight before the police could verify his identity. At last count, he jumped bail and is still on the run. With police resources severely reduced since the Great Crash, guys like him fall off the grid. Cops have shifted to a response mode rather than investigative mode.

"There's one last category we didn't discuss," said Callahan as the hour drew late one night in the Callahan kitchen.

"Remember the middle-aged, bald, angry white guy who chatted with me in the food court?"

"You're gonna have to narrow down the field, there's tons of angry old bald white guys," teased Sammy.

"This guy was a special case," said Callahan. "He spotted me as a fellow baby boomer. Figured he could connect with a kindred spirit. The initial conversation proved him right. We agreed on the gloomy weather and the sad state of world affairs. We agreed that kids today show less respect."

"So when did it go sour?" prompted Sammy.

"The conversation took a dark turn when this clown in his brown/green camouflage costume referred to the majority of patrons in the food court as animals. He predicted that, 'We have no future when "these people" take over and it'll come down to us versus them.' Guess who were 'these people' in the food court?" said Callahan.

"Dark skinned people speaking foreign languages," offered Butch.

"Exactly," said Callahan. "When did you become a sociologist?" quipped Callahan.

"When you became an accountant," shot back Butch. "Anyways, what did you do?"

"Well, I don't want to be standing next to this guy," said Callahan.

"Especially since from a distance, you guys could be twins," teased Sammy.

"So I made believe I just received a call from dispatch and had to rush off to it. I actually radioed dispatch to keep eyes on this renaissance man as he headed toward door number two.

"Dispatch radioed back after a few moments noting, 'Mr. Camo Man exited door number two without incident.'

"I was temporarily relieved but realized he'll be back and he's not alone. You all should keep an eye out for these time bombs. They come in all shapes, sizes, and colors," cautioned Callahan.

"No doubt he's a wack job, but it's the ugly, angry stares from very young children that worry me the most," commented Butch. "Their eyes send a message of total disdain and distrust for anyone wearing a uniform. Understandably, they and their elders experience bad interactions with authorities but those seeds of discontent were sown very deep."

"I had no idea that you thought that much about this," said Nicco.

"Damn right I think about this. I've been on the force long enough to see hate growing in the eyes of the young, old, black, white, everybody for that matter. I worry about where it's all going."

"So what's the bottom line, what should we be doing?" asked Nicco who was starting to have second thoughts about a cop career.

Advice spewed forth from veteran mall cops gathered around the table.

Butch said, "Watch your back and don't back down."

Callahan said, "But know when to back down and don't take stuff personally."

Ralph said, "Have a Plan B. Don't put all your eggs in one basket. Be ready to switch to another career."

A quietness descended upon this raucous group at this late hour. A blanket of silence always hovers when there are no clear solutions or good options.

Chapter 12:
Casseroles and Conversations

"Why are you watching that Kardashian crap?" said Callahan as he put his service belt away.

"It reminds me of my old college girlfriends," said Kevin.

Bryce hooted, "Me too."

"Yea, good luck with that, just don't bring 'em around here. I'd hate to scare 'em with big words and deep thoughts," said Callahan. "Switch to CNN, my brain's hungry. Speaking of hunger, that casserole smells great. Maggie, you're a magician in the kitchen."

"Hey, Dad, I have $300. With another $300 from you … maybe … I can build my own computer," interjected Bruce as he set plates without making eye contact with Callahan.

"Why not go to the store and buy a computer with a warranty like everybody else?" scoffed Callahan.

"Because everybody else pays too much. Plus building it myself will look good since I'm majoring in computer science. Did you know there's less chance the government can track me if I customize it?"

"Here we go again with big brother overlord talk," said Callahan, as he savored a mouthful of meatloaf washed down with Guinness. "Come to think of it, saving money, building a résumé, and keeping big brother at bay might be a good idea."

With that bit of business taken care of, Aunts Agnes and Helen stopped by as was their Friday night routine. They really were Callahan's aunts and they always had stories of working for the IRS and the hospital. Uncles Ralph and Butch also stopped by. Not real uncles but they earned this affectionate title because they were always there when it counted. Real stand up, no back down types of guys.

With more helpings of casseroles, the conversations turned to increased taxes and decreased benefits. Everybody was still reeling from the Great Compromise when benefits for everything were cut in half. Butch launched his litany, which Sammy could recite word for word. "Half your Social Security payments, double your taxes; Half your medical insurance benefits, double your co-payments."

Butch and Ralph predicted the time was coming when benefits would be cut further to only one-fourth. Butch sarcastically proclaimed, "We should be grateful for receiving half loaves. They just want us to shut up."

Everybody around the table chimed in with their own troublesome story.

Callahan recalled a former job where they arbitrarily cut his salary by $20,000. He said, "When I asked if the pay cut would reduce my hours to part-time, they non-chalantly said no. Less money, more work, same hours, and no thanks for years of good service. Welcome to working in an 'at-will' state." Callahan loved to mock this phrase, saying, "The company has the right to dump you for no cause and you have the right to leave the company. Well I would hope so," he grumbled. Adding insult to injustice, Callahan recalled how he brought his $500 Christmas bonus check to the bank at the end of that year. "When the perky teller at the bank in her red and green Frosty the Snowman sweater exclaimed, 'How nice,' I let her know that the other $19,500 was missing. Without missing a beat or hearing a word, she chirped, 'Happy holidays! Is there anything else I can help you with today?'

"Ho, ho, ho, and no," mumbled Callahan who grew increasingly impatient with that insincere departure tagline.

Others chimed in with their own horror stories. The names and circumstances differed, but the common theme was erosion of the working class.

Younger members of the extended family soaked up the stories. They resolved to do what they could and not get screwed. There was talk of underground economies where cash is king and no records are kept. There was talk of attending an upcoming rally to protest the additional cuts that Ralph and Butch predicted. Callahan encouraged activism. However, he cautioned that sometimes it's better to think long distance rather than sprint. Maybe that's why he was known as the turtle. He was a plodder, not a sprinter. He encouraged blending in, building alliances and gaining intel. He exhorted his kitchen cabinet to be what's known as tan-man.

Everybody knew what he was talking about.

When not in his mall cop uniform, Callahan dressed in bland neutral colors, mostly tan and beige. This wasn't because he was colorblind. He was simply indifferent to styles or fads. He told everybody that the more bland and innocuous the tones, the easier it was to chat with others. Successfully chatting down a potential foe can provide valuable info. When others speak freely, bridges can be built. Alliances can be formed among newfound friends. Fences can keep foes at bay. Callahan called this his survival mechanism in the post-9/11, post-Great Crash era. It served the extended family well when they were forced to deal with the outside world. These rigorous conversations around casseroles served Sammy well when he had flashbacks while scoring points a few years later, on the debate team at Oxford University.

Dinner conversations over casseroles usually started with the absurd and evolved into the humorous. The mall provided an abundance of both. The absurd included shoppers spending money they didn't have. Initially, everyone around the table chuckled but a quietness descended when Callahan asked, "Who among you has mortgages, car loans, credit card debts, and student loans?"

Recent college grads Kevin and Bryce asked, "Are we nothing more than highly educated indentured servants?"

Callanan explained, "Our ancestors had nothing but the clothes on their backs when they came to America to get a fresh start."

Kevin asked, "Where can I go to get my fresh start?" Again, silence around the table.

Uncle Butch mentioned he had connections way up in Vermont near the Canadian border. He asked, "Who's up for forming a commune up north? We could grow our own food, rig up a water wheel on a stream that runs through the property, and heat the cabin with wood burning stoves."

"I've visited the site many times," commented Uncle Ralph. "Great place for hunting and remote enough for target shooting any time you want, not like down here where you have to pay membership fees for everything."

"I'm OK with paying for the range, I just don't like hearing everybody's politics when I shoot. I can't even go to the gym anymore without somebody questioning my party and my patriotism," complained Callahan.

"Let's get back to my original idea of a commune up north," continued Butch.

"You got to stop using that word, commune," said Ralph. "Especially since you refer to your blogs as manifestos. Next thing you know, they'll round us up as socialists and communists. Next stop Gitmo. By the way, is that place still open? Are they taking reservations?"

"Let's worry about Gitmo some other time," said Callahan. "For now let's test out this idea of shared labor and shared resources. We can take an inventory of equipment. We have snow blowers, plows, ride on lawn mowers, and chainsaws, just to name a few. We have pickup trucks with trailers to lug the equipment around and do odd jobs for cash. No need to tell the tax man."

"If cash doesn't work, there's also bartering for services," added Sammy.

"Let's just try this for a couple of seasons to see how this works out. We could plow snow in winter, rake/mulch leaves in fall, plant gardens in spring, harvest and preserve the produce to get us through the winter," said Sammy who was getting more on board with this off-the-grid concept.

"Cutting grass in the summer will keep the health department at bay," said Callahan as he thumbed through a stack of bills. "I got fined twice last year. Why the hell do I bother cutting the grass? It doesn't produce anything. The backyard could be converted to vegetable gardens."

"Why not plant crops in the front yard?" poked Ralph, knowing full well the answer.

"One big reason, Maggie. She's gonna want that grassy curb appeal. Hey, maybe I can have some sheep out there and I can get back to my Irish roots," said Callahan with a devilish grin. "Seriously though," he continued, "while we're sharing equipment, we can also share skills. Get everyone cross-trained in the use of power tools. Volunteer on Habitat for Humanity crews. Do some good while preparing for Armageddon."

"I see where we're going with this. Help others, help each other, hunker down, and brace ourselves from the haters," said Sammy.

"Now you're all getting the picture," said Callahan with the air of Robin Hood addressing his band of merry men.

Chapter 13:
Crazy Conversations, Crazy Times

Never a dull moment at the Callahan house. People and cars came and went at all hours. Callahan loved to say, "Keeps burglars guessing." He was always rushing off to one of his three jobs.

Maggie worked all hours as a bookkeeper. As the years piled up, so did layoff notices. She never missed a chance to warn others to avoid bookkeeping jobs at the start of the tax season. She said, "They promise permanent employment, then April 15th arrives and they say sayonara. Thanks for nothing. Oh well, at least they'll always need bookkeepers," said the eternally optimistic Maggie.

"Don't put all your eggs in that basket," cautioned Callahan. "If they can make trucks self-driving, what's to say bookkeepers go out of style like telephone operators?"

Sammy was half-listening to these old timers banter and asked, "What's a telephone operator?"

Knowing Sammy and Bruce's affinity for *Star Wars*, Callahan bellowed, "A long time ago, in a galaxy far, far away, people did things all by themselves. They even thought for themselves. All done without today's click-ety clacking apps."

The Callahan household wasn't just busy. It was eccentric and downright scary to the uninitiated. Mannequins discarded from the mall were scattered throughout the backyard. Some were dismembered. Most were disfigured. Arrows pierced their hearts, victims of archery contests. Faces were splattered with red paint, victims of paintball battles. Bullet holes in chests were convincing deterrents to would-be burglars. Bryce liked to say as he practiced archery, "Those who hunt when the sun goes down become the hunted when they venture onto the Callahan property."

A severed Styrofoam head found on a nearby dead-end street perched on the two remaining slats of an Adirondack chair leaning against the front door. Callahan liked to say, "Nice, successful people decorate their entryways with potted red geraniums. Not the Callahans."

Broken windows of the garage never got fixed after vandals struck on Halloween night some years ago. This was the same night Callahan and his kids ran down the street with sickles and bats in hand. As luck would have it, for all parties concerned, the scoundrels were never found.

Overgrown shrubs and the horribly cracked driveway all cried out for routine maintenance.

Times had changed (and not for the better) but Fort Callahan remained a decrepit but fortified bastion.

Mayhem on the exterior was matched by conversational mayhem at the dinner table. In between mounds of beef stroganoff topped with corn, conversations went like this:

Callahan exclaimed, "Everybody should be issued a grenade."

Maggie sighed, "And your point is?"

Callahan responded, "Self-defense. Kill them before they kill us."

Maggie prodded, "And who are they?"

Callahan shouted, "Everybody, terrorists, mass shooters, enemies both foreign and domestic, all nut cases."

Bryce never missed an opportunity to see how far Callahan would unravel. He asked, "How old should you be to get a grenade?"

"The younger the better," said Callahan, "especially with these school shooter maniacs."

Claire ventured, "You should get some help if you're having these thoughts."

Callahan responded, "I'm dead serious and you'll all be dead if you don't follow my advice. Why not give these nuts a quick way out. If they're thinking of killing a bunch of innocent people, they can go out in a blaze of glory. Isn't that what they want anyways?"

Claire sighed, "I know where this is going. I've heard this song before."

"Damn right you have," said Callahan. "This ties in perfectly with the Kevorkian Foundation."

Claire rolled her eyes saying, "Here we go again with Kevorkian."

Rookie Nicco asked, "Who the hell is Kevorkian?"

Kevin groaned, "Don't get him started."

Callahan explained, "Kevorkian was known as Dr. Death some years ago. He proposed assisted suicide for the terminally ill. I say, take it to the next level and include the nut cases."

"And how will you get these nuts to do such a nutty thing?" asked Sammy who loved to grovel in the weeds with Callahan.

"Let's do some public service announcements," said Callahan, waving his arms as if rolling out a party platform at a national convention. "They could go like this:

Feel like hurting others for no reason?
Want to kill innocent people?
Start with yourself.
Go out in a blaze of glory.
Be the guy that takes no prisoners.
Be the guy who won't back down."

"I told you we shouldn't get him started," said Claire. "And you think ramping up a psycho killer is a solution?"

Bruce pulled away from his laptop saying, "Hey, I'm a game developer and he might have something here. The nut could enter a virtual reality arena. Once inside, he gets killed for real. Then everybody else gets killed virtually. No more nut and the rest of us stay safe. I like it."

"Down the rabbit hole we go," said Claire.

Bruce gave her a brotherly poke, saying, "You're the movie producer, you should be on board with this."

Callahan rolled back in his chair, hands clasped behind his head exclaiming, "I'm glad somebody appreciates my genius. By the way, how do you know

I'm not gonna be the one that snaps? I could be the mass shooter. After all, I didn't get the nickname snapping turtle for nothing."

"Here we go again with you and mass shooters," said Bryce. "Why are you so hung up with them?"

"Do I have to remind you that I'm a mall cop? Need I remind you that malls are soft targets? Shooters are random. They take innocent lives. Why don't these cowardly bastards have the balls to hunt down those who screwed them? That's what I would do. I got my list. I bet everybody here keeps a list in their head," said Callahan, slowly pointing his finger in a half circle to everyone in the kitchen.

"Don't you realize there was way more crime back in the Dark Ages?" countered Bryce. "Jolly old England wasn't so jolly." Bryce was a physicist who liked to crunch numbers and tinker with inventions but, like Callahan, he had an appreciation for the arc of history.

Sammy was absorbed in this verbal mayhem. After a pause in the frenetic discourse, he said, "You had enough common sense to raise me. It got you this far so why stop now?"

Callahan was winding down at this point and acquiesced saying, "Guess you're right. Maybe we could issue everybody a taser instead of a grenade. See, I'm willing to compromise. Hey, look at the time, I need my beauty rest."

To which they all too quickly agreed that it was way past Callahan's bedtime.

The next morning, everybody awoke to the aroma of bacon sizzling in the pan and pancakes stacked high on a platter on the kitchen table. Maggie picked up where she left off the night before, barking orders to everyone who ventured into the kitchen. "Set the table and find my favorite spatula," was her common refrain, since nothing in the congested household ever got returned to its original spot. In the kitchen, Maggie was like a surgeon in the emergency room ordering technicians to fetch tools.

Callahan managed to slink past the kitchen doorway, avoiding dreaded kitchen duty so he could engage in his favorite pastime of writing and blogging. He typed as quietly and quickly as possible. Today he added an article to his "Manifesto of Big Ideas". His notepad was a jumble of descriptions of suspected shoplifters interspersed with ideas that popped into his head during a mall shift. "There it is," he muttered as he stumbled onto the last page.

His mind was racing as his fingers were typing. If we can have foreign exchange students, why can't we have domestic exchange students? It might cut down on the haters if we spent time in each other's neighborhoods. Might learn something about each other. Why does it have to be just students? Maybe some of us old dogs can learn some new tricks. But then again, thought Callahan as he suspended his typing, old habits are hard to break. Haters got to be haters. I know they say that travel is the antidote to prejudice. But then again, I got friends and family who traveled all over and only came back hating all the more.

Callahan was so deep in his mental machinations that he didn't notice Sammy pulling up a chair next to him.

Sammy haltingly asked, "Can I ask you about something?"

"Sure, what?" said Callahan as he stopped typing but kept viewing his screen.

"You know how sometimes I hang out at the Gallaghers' on Friday nights after swim practice."

"Yea, the Gallaghers, nice Irish family. Live on the other side of the parkway. Lace curtain Irish. Fancy house with everything in its place. Dining rooms loaded with fine china. Is that what's bothering you? The likes of us shanty Irish frolicking with them?"

"No, it's not your class warfare spiel. It's just that, I don't know, they seem to like me but maybe not that much."

"What do you mean? What's not to like?"

"I get invited to stuff but I'm not sure if they really want me. And, it's not just them. I get that feeling in other places."

"What makes you say that?"

"Kids' parents don't mind if I pal around with the group. But I get a look if I do something with their daughter."

"What kind of something are you talking about?"

"I'm not talking about fooling around, I'm just talking about being alone with a girl."

"Gallagher's got a couple of daughters around your age as I recall. Beautiful girls."

"Yea, Maggie's a sophomore and Katelyn's in my senior year. Their dad sits by the center island in their kitchen. He looks into the den while we're watching TV. I can feel his stare on the back of my Afro."

"So you haven't seen him stare, you just get this sixth sense feeling."

"Sounds paranoid but I do. And it's not just there. I get that feeling in stores and even when we go to church."

"Imagine that, being un-Christian and prejudiced even in God's house."

"I'm serious, don't you get that feeling when we go somewhere and they're trying to figure out what's the deal with me?"

"I know. I see the stare when they think I'm not looking. But you know something else?"

"What's that?"

"I got no answer. What you're talking about goes a long way back. It's not gonna change anytime soon, especially where there's white girls concerned."

"I get it. Stay cool, be cool."

"Can I give you some more advice?" offered Callahan as he shut off his computer, removing his glasses and rubbing his eyes.

"Fire away, you know I hang on your every word," said Sammy.

"What we're talking about here is staying in your lane. Make sure you look before you change lanes. Every once in a while, you're gonna get sideswiped," said Callahan, stroking his mustache.

"So when have you changed lanes?" asked Sammy.

"One time I went out to dinner with a black girl."

"Does Maggie know this?"

"Don't worry about Maggie, this was way before I met her. I bumped into this girl who used to live in my college dorm. We went to dinner in a fancy restaurant. I think we got stares but then again maybe it was all in my mind. It happened a long time ago. I try not to live too much in the world of 'wooda, cooda, shooda'."

"So was it a date?" pressed Sammy.

"I really don't know. She was nice but I never followed up. To this day, I always wondered why not."

"Maybe that voice in your head kept saying, 'Stay in your lane'," said Sammy.

"Maybe so," mused Callahan. Old relationships and near misses cascaded through his mind, none of which he dared share with Sammy.

"I'm just gonna go for a run, clear my head," announced Sammy, breaking the silence that follows conversations which dance around the edges of the unspoken.

"No pancakes and bacon? Maggie's gonna be disappointed," said Callahan.

"Can't slow me down, I'll eat later," said Sammy as he stepped toward the doorway in his tracksuit.

"OK. And hey, be careful out there," warned Callahan.

Chapter 14:
Bumper Stickers and Coats of Arms

Common conversations around the dinner table were the usual, "What happened today?" Catch-up conversations were a lost art in other households. If anyone was at a loss for words in Callahan's kitchen, recounting bumper stickers observed during patrols offered food for thought. Bumper stickers can be insightful, provocative, hateful, perplexing, and humorous. Matching them with license plates and vehicle models can profile the driver's likes, dislikes, and even their outlook on life. Callahan and Sammy frequently played this profiling game, describing drivers without actually meeting them.

Sammy kicked off the conversation observing, "School mascots are a sure sign of brainiacs or jocks or both."

Uncle Ralph, who never went to college on a football scholarship thanks to a high school knee injury, ruefully sneered, "They must be rich bastards."

Kevin, fresh out of college and starting the loan repayment journey quipped, "If they're like me, say goodbye to dreams and hello to slavery."

Callahan, ever the curmudgeon, couldn't resist ragging on cars loaded down with stickers announcing vacation trips. He said he recently teased a perky middle-aged woman in a Honda Odyssey minivan commenting, "You need a bigger car 'cause the tailgate's so cluttered with stickers. She's just another announcer," he grumbled as he fished for another piece of kielbasa swimming in the pot. Everybody knew what he meant and braced for another Callahan rant.

With Christmas approaching, Callahan scoffed at people who send holiday year-in-review greetings detailing spectacular accomplishments of their perfect families. "Gets under my skin with their exotic vacation spots, high honors, and breaking sports records. All soaked in self-satisfaction."

"Maybe they just want to share their lives with you, like normal people," offered Claire who considered a career in counseling after years of installing guardrails on Callahan's comments.

"I'm just fed up with postcards brimming with happy faces, pets in costumes staged in immaculate homes or on beaches in paradise. You know what I'm gonna do this Christmas?"

"I'm afraid to know but spit it out, don't hold back," coaxed Claire.

"I'm gonna mail a year-in-review that'll knock the socks off those phony bastards. It'll include announcements of felony arrests, misdemeanors, psychiatric commitments, and bankruptcies."

"At the rate we're going, maybe that stuff won't be so fake," said Kevin as he perused job advertisements searching for higher pay to pay off student loans.

"Every year Maggie rounds us up after Christmas for the photo in front of that goddamned tree. It's a pain in the ass to put it up only to take it down."

"Bah humbug," interjected Sammy who was still young enough to appreciate Christmas traditions.

"How about a Christmas family photo with all of us clad in orange jumpsuits posing in front of an abandoned building in BellHaven. The caption could read 'One more payment and we own it!' Now that would be fun!"

Uncle Butch was nursing a brandy when he recalled his favorite bumper stickers. "One said 'University of Saigon'. Must be a Vietnam Vet."

"How about the one that said 'College of Hard Knocks'? Obviously someone who had been there, done that."

"Last but not least, there was the 'Starfleet Academy', obviously a Trekkie."

Everyone got a chuckle from the humorous ones. However, the increasingly crusty Callahan observed, "There's an uptick in stickers of angry people venting about a politician or spewing venom over their favorite issue. I remember when campaign stickers used to be positive endorsements about a candidate. Now they spew poison at each other."

"Not to mention promising the world before the election and delivering nothing afterward," added Uncle Butch.

"They can promise all they want," said Callahan. "I'm more worried about the ultra-angry, ultra-frustrated bumper stickers. Mark my words, they're the predictors of a mass shooting. I've been patrolling parking lots for over fifteen years and I don't like what I'm seeing."

Another night of doom and gloom, thought Sammy but he kept his mouth shut, having learned years ago that it's unwise to interrupt Callahan once he jumped on his soap box.

Dinner was finished but unlike most households where members scatter once the food has been wolfed down, members of the Callahan clan lingered, savoring dessert, discussions, and liquor. Maggie placed a plate of freshly baked brownies in the middle of the massive oak table with the admonishment to, "Save some for tomorrow."

Callahan's kitchen was a mixing pot of visitors of all ages and perspectives. Claire nicknamed the kitchen "the bus depot". Regulars had their own designated cups, mugs, and beer steins. Maggie, the queen of the manor, had her teacup displaying the Korean flag. She purchased tchotchke from every gift shop she frequented. This cup was a fond memory of the day she and Sammy brought themselves up to speed on Korean history and culture when they visited the Korean Museum in New York City.

Uncle Ralph waited for the head of his Sam Adams beer to settle in his commemorative Tom Brady retirement stein. Ralph was a loyal New Englander through and through. All his teams were Boston based and he was not one to jump ship during losing seasons. Staring into his amber brew, he said, "Some bumper stickers beg the question, so what? Take, for example, the ones that say, 'This car climbed Mt. Washington'. All that tells me is that it tacked on a whole lot of useless miles."

"Yea," said Uncle Butch who added, "who cares if your car went 'south of the border'."

"And what about the ones that tell you 'My kid's an honor student'. OK, I'm happy for you and your kid but what's this got to do with me?" said Ralph, still harboring resentment about not going to college.

"I'm a glass half empty type of guy," said Callahan as he refilled his own glass of Guinness. "Now Claire, she's a glass half full gal."

"You got that right, I try to focus on positive stickers like LOVE, PEACE, JOY. You know, stuff that hopefully everybody can support," said Claire.

"If only people would practice what they preach," said Maggie, looking up from a magazine describing a casserole recipe.

"Well, I guess peace and love stickers are better than driving to job interviews with a war and hate sticker," suggested Callahan.

"Just like the THUG LIFE T-shirts people wear in the mall," remarked Butch. "I can't believe the gangster crap people prance around in. I better not see that on you, young man," he said as Sammy scrolled through notifications on his iPhone.

"No, sir," responded Sammy without looking up, nonchalantly assuring him that he was a student of the Callahan School of Fashion.

"Being Tan-Man gets you intel and keeps you alive," advised Callahan. "Keep the colors muted, the opinions to yourself, and the weapons concealed. That's how you weave your way around the nuts in society."

"I love the way we go from bumper stickers to fashion to Armageddon," said Claire, seeking a conversational exit ramp since the hour was getting late.

Callahan took the cue. He announced a lightning round of suggested bumper stickers starting with "Target Shooting Liberal" to which Butch responded, "Why do they think you're a pussy if just want feed and clothe people?"

"You've turned into a real humanitarian," teased Ralph.

"Don't get me wrong, I still support the saying 'do the crime, do the time'," shot back Butch.

Sammy had been quietly scrolling the news feed announcing the latest acquittals of a gaggle of senators caught profiting from insider trading. He shouted out, "Big shots get pass, peasants get kick in ass!"

"I like that," said Ralph who was quick to add, "Welfare cheats and hedge fund bandits: Save space, share a jail cell."

"I like the concept but it's a bit long for a bumper sticker," commented Maggie with the practicality of a bookkeeper.

"How about, 'health care makes me sick and want to die,'" shouted Ralph whose wife's multiple sclerosis was advancing while her co-payments were increasing.

"Dying's the only way we get to screw those bastards," exclaimed Callahan who immediately regretted the comment on the heels of Ralph's wife's illness.

His guilt was short-lived. They were too amped up to connect that dot.

"In the old days, they didn't have bumper stickers but they had coats of arms," said Callahan as he gazed upon the Callahan coat of arms suspended over the doorway of the kitchen.

"Of course they didn't have bumper stickers, they didn't have cars," said the ever-practical Maggie.

"The way the world's going, Callahan & Company needs a coat of arms. Something that shouts, 'Don't tread on me'," said Callahan.

"Your coat of arms has an eagle but it needs to be more aggressive," said Sammy.

"How about having one of the eagle talons crushing the head of Mr. Banker Man, you know that business character from the Monopoly game," said Butch.

"The other talon could be crushing the head of the bandit character, you know that masked figure on the Monopoly game," added Ralph.

"I like it. Sticking it to the rich bastards and street punks," said Callahan. "Hey, Claire, can you work up some T-shirts using that photoshop magic you do?"

"Sure," said Claire without looking up from her iPhone. She suggested that Bruce, who was not present, could include this aggressive coat of arms in his video games.

Tuckered out from ragging on the state of world affairs, so ended another night of food, fun and mayhem in Callahan's kitchen.

Chapter 15:
Respect

Life's monotonous drumbeat thumped on. While the kids got taller inside Callahan's household, tempers on the street got shorter. Callahan and sidekick Sammy's interactions with the public reflected global warming of temperaments.

The following episode best exemplifies caustic tempers.

Callahan approached the fire lane by the Target store with amber lights flashing on his security truck. With a beep of the horn, a souped-up Honda Civic with a spoiler on the trunk and oversized shiny chrome hubcaps sped away, blasting an angry rap song. That's when Callahan saw a tall, gangly white male in a sleeveless white T-shirt standing on the sidewalk. Next to him was a giant German shepherd. This was the Arnold Schwarzenegger of German (maybe Austrian) shepherds. As Callahan exited the truck, he saw a red Buick sedan parked on the bright yellow hash marks of the no parking area. The vehicle had numerous bumper stickers but the bright orange one with the black scorpion and a raised stinger exclaiming "Don't Mess With Me" shouted the loudest at Callahan. I bet that's Mr. Dog Owner's car, thought Callahan. His hunch was confirmed when he heard, "Yea, that's mine." As Callahan approached, the dog owner assured him that he would be moving soon since his daughter and son were shopping in Target. Callahan thought to himself, everybody's an exception, at least in their own mind.

What was wrong about this picture was the fact that the German shepherd was not on a leash. The owner allowed him to roam freely in a circle four feet away from his master. Patrons attempting to enter Target gingerly walked in an arc rather than taking their chances. Instead of leading off with his security guard speech, Callahan complimented him on this magnificent creature. He really was an impressive dog, albeit menacing.

Callahan mentioned that his uncle John was the K-9 trainer for the Providence police department. He recounted Uncle John's opinion that Dobermans were a bit too smart for their own good. When they saw a gun they backed down while the shepherds were all business and showed no fear. Mr. Dog Owner liked this story. He figured that he and Callahan were kindred spirits, maybe even on the level of Band of Brothers. This led to his comment as a Latino family passed by that, "This country is goin' to hell in a handbasket. Soon we'll all need attack dogs to keep them at bay."

Maybe the family heard his comment, maybe not. Callahan knew that it was time for law enforcement. He mentioned that dogs need to be leashed if they are on the property, as required by local ordinance. He affably mentioned that an unleashed dog might make patrons nervous and that's bad for business. Callahan figured that appealing to this guy's red-blooded, all-American support of capitalism would seal the deal and leash the dog. Instead, Mr. Dog Owner became indignant and stated, "It's a free country and Americus is never leashed." The director of security happened to come by and reiterated the need to leash the dog.

With this second opinion, the dog owner grumbled about his rights and liberties but he complied and moseyed over to his car with the dog in tow. The honeymoon between two older, balding white guys was over. Compliance was achieved but Callahan could sense rage building up in this guy who spent a lifetime bucking authority. He noticed as he sauntered away that the tattoo on his left forearm had that same damn scorpion exclaiming "Don't Mess With Me". He recalled that the tattoo on his right forearm said "Respect: It's Earned".

Callahan thought to himself, how can a guy who is so obsessed with getting respect not find it in his heart to respect others? Besides sticking up for Americus's Bill of Rights, he boasted about his rental properties being cash cows. He lamented about how he could be richer if only the government kept its hand out of his pocket. Why do knuckleheads always have to mention, for no reason, how rich they are and why the government is screwing up their pursuit of happiness? Did the sight of his uniform trigger some visceral need to start a class war? Why does he act like he's lord of the manor with his trusty steed instilling fear and demanding respect from the lowly peasants?

Callahan happened to know the Latino family that passed by. They worked their asses off building up a landscaping business and they regularly shopped at the mall. But, of course, Mr. Dog Owner was unaware of that. For that matter, he had no idea of how screwed up Callahan's life was.

As the guy's son and daughter emerged from shopping, loaded down with purchases, they piled into the red Buick. Disgruntled dog owner barked to his tween son, "Steffan, get your worthless ass in the car," following up with the customary smack on his head. With a revving up of the eight-cylinder clunker, they sped off from the restricted parking space. Callahan radioed to the dispatcher, "Mobile to Dispatch … take CT registration … AC-1776 … that's Alfa-Charlie 1776."

Dispatch responded ten-four and Callahan asked that the registration be logged for possible future reference. He had a feeling this type of guy might snap if he feels that he's not sufficiently RESPECTED. The irony of the plate number 1776 was not lost on Callahan. Back in 1776 there were real patriots fighting for freedom. Now, thought Callahan, we have angry, unhappy shoppers and wannabe patriots. What also caught the attention of both Callahan and Sammy, who had joined him for the balance of the evening shift, was the threatening manner that the son pointed a super-soaker gun in their direction. Granted, he's just a kid and it's only a souped-up water gun, but there was something about the way he pointed it and his hateful stare that triggered a gut sense of concern.

So much for "Respect, It's Earned".

The Buick was long gone. The shift ended about an hour later. Thankfully, this was the only negative interaction on what would normally be a feisty Friday night. While on duty all mall cops avoid using the phrase "it's quiet tonight" for fear of jinxing themselves. While Callahan was decompressing over a Guinness down at Willy's Water Hole, he was still obsessing over his interaction with the belligerent dog owner and his dysfunctional family.

Lately his mind kept playing the same thought, why does everybody generally get along as long as:

- the topics remain superficial.
- you're not asking much, if anything, of the other person.
- the mood is upbeat with either a smile or humor or both.

People can be a pain in the ass sometimes, thought Callahan, but deep down I enjoy the interactions with the public. Hell, this is what has kept me coming back year after year. During brief conversations with patrons helping them find their vehicles, a local guy like me gets to travel the world. I've met Bobbies from London, former Green Berets, exchange students from the Middle East and people from every walk of life. It's been a fun ride but society's gotten so polarized after the Great Crash and the Great Compromise. Cutbacks on Social Security, Medicare and Medicaid got us all sitting on our last nerve. I'm sick of the discordant discourse. I'm starting to question everybody's motives. Who can be trusted anymore? The happy-go-lucky days of all for one and one for all have become distant memories.

His melancholy moment was interrupted when he was joined by Sammy, Claire, Bryce, Bruce, and Kevin for a traditional regrouping at Willy's Water Hole. Story-telling can enlighten others while the storyteller exhales. Tonight, like so many nights, was one of enlightenment. One-liners jumped from topic to topic interspersed with verbal jabs laced with Irish wit. At least we still have each other, thought Callahan as he leaned back precariously in his captain's chair.

Chapter 16:
The Winds of Change

Bellhaven continued its downward spiral. Northville was a mature suburb showing its age. So was Callahan. No longer did he bound up stairwells or practice lunges walking down service corridors. But when patrolling public areas, he showed no sign of fatigue. To show fear is to be intimidated. When a bunch of young Turks with big attitudes were escorted out, one asked, "You scared?"

Callahan's monotone response was, "No, just tired, this is my third job." Actually, he was scared. Wannabes looking to get street creds as gangsters can be volatile. Callahan's calm facade of disinterest was a defensive strategy that served him well. Getting an aggressor off topic and humanizing the conversation is a form of verbal sparring that avoids actual sparring. Sammy was a quick student who mastered this technique in stressful situations. He enjoyed keeping others guessing while building trust and assimilating in social circumstances. His mixed race and multicultural upbringing encouraged conversations with those interested in conversing. The incessant question "what are you?" sometimes got under his skin.

"I'm tired of being a mixed breed dog. Why can't I be a thoroughbred? Seems like that's what people want," he used to complain to Callahan.

Callahan counseled him saying, "I'm proud of my Irish heritage but being a mongrel has its advantages. Did you notice they're the smartest dogs that live the longest? That reminds me, remember the time that nosy patron asked if you were from India?"

"Yea, that was fun," admitted Sammy, who recalled how she was eavesdropping while Callahan and Sammy chatted in Gaelic. "I convinced her in my best Indian accent that I was a police cadet visiting from Mumbai sent to America to learn policing tactics."

"Irish wit to the rescue," said Callahan as he delivered a fatherly pat on Sammy's back.

On mall patrols, wit and mindfulness are valuable tools of the trade. But having Wild Bill in your corner is a reassuring Plan B. Wild Bill had military experience but details were murky and mysterious. What was clear was his ability to tear a person apart. Having him as your wingman was comforting. What was most disturbing was the sense that he would enjoy an opportunity to quarter someone. Living in an abandoned house with no running water, no heat, and growing up in public housing turned Wild Bill into a formidable foe. Callahan kidded him because only he could sit through a life-saving CPR class while sketching bomb-making illustrations.

Speaking of CPR, there was Billy the EMT wannabe. If there was any type of emergency response class, he signed up for it in hopes of joining an EMT crew or a fire department. Great kid by any standards. He was the kind of kid you want your sister or daughter to meet. Billy and Callahan often shared the lunchroom. He was always ready to apply the Heimlich maneuver when Callahan coughed while eating. Callahan repeatedly assured him that coughing while eating was annoying but not life threatening. Billy backed off from applying a life-saving choke hold, but the thought that Callahan was not himself lingered with him.

As Callahan changed and aged, so did the mall. The housekeeping department had to scramble to place buckets and gondolas to catch rain that leaked through skylights. Other more high-tech malls in affluent areas were retrofitted with elaborate security measures. They could electronically cordon off areas, effectively isolating active shooters. The advantage of such a quarantine was to limit the level of carnage. These expensive force shield systems were comparable to prisons where units could be isolated when rioting erupted. The downside to this system was the Hobbesian choice that had to be made. Would a few innocents be taken hostage and most likely killed for the sake of saving the many? Times changed and the preponderance of lone wolf maniacs and partisan warriors necessitated draconian measures. Because Renaissance Center was not experiencing a renaissance, high technology security was not in the cards.

When Callahan & Company regrouped after work at Willy's Water Hole, conversations usually started with the usual Yankees versus Red Sox. After a few beers, conversations moved to more ominous discussions concerning the future of the mall. Like factory workers of prior generations discussing the closing of the plant, mall cops discussed the demise of the mall.

Big Jack, the director of security, announced, "In some West Coast industrial parks they're using robots to circulate through the complex. Drones armed with cameras and audio capability are tracking intruders. Facial recognition is verifying who's good and who's bad at every entrance."

"Wish we had that stuff," groaned the group in unison. Big Jack cautioned them to, "Be careful what you wish for, it might put us all out of a job."

"I'm no city planner," said Butch, "but working the mall day in and day out, I see trends. You want to hear some recommendations?"

"What were you thinking?" asked Callahan, who really had been a city planner in his earlier career but made it a habit to not show his cards up front.

"Well, the fad stores are just that, they come and go. The tech stores thrive. The eateries make big splashes at grand openings, then level off," said Butch.

"I see the handwriting on the wall," added Ralph. "See how the big anchor stores tried to be all things to all people and now look at 'em. Droppin' like flies."

"Where's Robert Moses when you need him?" asked Callahan, knowing full well that nobody knew who the hell Robert Moses was.

Junior took the bait as he so often did during discussions. He piped up commenting, "That's the guy who parted the Red Sea and killed all those Egyptians. That was cool."

"Not quite, my friend," said Callahan with the patience of a saint. "Robert Moses was the guy who designed all the expressways that weave in and out of New York City. That was back in the day when you could steamroll projects actually getting things done. Maybe I could be the Robert Moses of America's malls."

Oh boy, thought Sammy, here we go with Callahan's delusions of grandeur. Sometimes he thinks he's Napoleon, he's even built like him.

Another round of drinks and all sorts of ideas spilled forth.

Callahan suggested mosh pits with mud wrestling. Sammy teased with the question, "Have you ever been in a mosh pit and for that matter have you ever been to a concert?"

"Yea, wise guy, I went to concerts in high school when my buddy Frank worked at the WPOOP radio station. Free tickets, so there!"

"How about red-light districts?" suggested Butch, looking over to Captain Wheeler with a devilish grin.

"Don't look at me just because I was stationed in Amsterdam. But come to think of it, taxing prostitution and pot kept the streets clean and the potholes filled," responded Wheeler who always seemed to grasp the bigger picture.

"Why don't we just set aside an area where the assholes could live like they do at home. They could litter, vandalize, and fight to their heart's content. We could call it the Free Behavior Zone," said Big Jack who had grown a thick skin of cynicism after years as Mall Security Director.

"Some of them are neat, clean, and respectable at home but they come here to shit on us," countered Butch who liked to take a contrarian position just to get a rise out of the others. Sometimes, however, he really meant what he said.

"I've worked in public housing projects and sat in some very neat living rooms. The problem is that outside the apartment all hell breaks loose," agreed Callahan. "The kids we're dealing with aren't Rhode Scholars but I got to believe that some of them could make something of themselves. Instead, they all seem to be dummying each other down."

"Just take everybody one at a time," offered Butch who on this occasion seemed to really mean it.

"Mall cops are not economists, so what do we know? Well, I'll tell you what I know," said Callahan, answering his own question. "We need mixed use. Don't put all our eggs in one basket."

"So what are you suggesting?" asked Butch.

Callahan responded, "Retail produces nothing, but inventing and manufacturing actually creates stuff. What's our other options? Car washes, dollar stores, pawn shops, and tattoo shops? What have we got to lose? We got enough of that crap already in BellHaven."

"I love to tinker and experiment," jumped in Bryce. "Why don't we have a discovery center where kids could have fun while learning? We could have an innovation center that both creates and entertains. We could have a catwalk over the workshop. People love to see things getting made, like touring a bakery, winery, or a brewery."

Thoughts of a winery and brewery brought applause around the table. "I'm up for some free samples," said Butch.

"Who knows, maybe kids would be inspired to become scientists and inventors," said Bryce who could not give up the notion of making stuff rather than buying stuff.

History buff Captain Wheeler reminded the group that, "It was Yankee ingenuity that made this region famous, why can't we do it again?"

Sammy added, "The observation deck over the workshop could be like looking down on Santa's workshop. Don't forget it's a mall. Toys and presents are still our bread and butter."

"Speaking of bread and butter," said Butch, "push that Irish soda bread over my way."

"What's the number one rule of realtors?" asked Callahan, knowing the answer based upon years working in real estate and property management. "It's location, economy of scale, critical mass, and a sense of excitement. You need to create a buzz that makes the mall a destination point," he said without skipping a beat..

"Let's have some high-rises, skywalks with moving sidewalks, fountains, and light shows at night. If my proposal is accepted, the Renaissance Center would rank among the world's cities such as London, Paris, and Dubai."

Members of his kitchen cabinet sighed in unison, wondering if somebody had slipped something into his drink.

"Ahh, the plans we can concoct after a few beers," said Butch. "Who knew us mall cops are planners and dreamers?"

"Unfortunately, we're also canaries in the mine," said Callahan with a remorseful swig of his beer.

During lunch breaks, Callahan would reminisce with fellow mall cops while Sammy was within ear shot doing either homework or job shadowing. Older mall cops missed the good old days when upward of a hundred rowdy youths on a Saturday night were ejected for misbehaving. The rookie cops yearned for a taste of action that would embellish their law enforcement resume. Callahan cautioned both veterans and rookies that as bad as the bad old days sounded, it was preferable to the sullen, nihilistic mood of today's youngsters. He reminded them that, "Back when youth could act out and clown around, it was like a safety valve on a high pressure pipe releasing pent up anger by alienated youths."

"I know what you mean," chimed in both Butch and Ralph. "We've seen it in the stares of young black kids. It's in the stares of skinhead kids, the white-trash offspring."

Sammy interrupted, reminding "It's no longer cool to refer to people as white trash. If they're the bottom rung of the ladder, then what am I supposed to be?"

"I'm just sayin' that you can be dirt poor whether you're black or white or whatever. There's always been poor people. It's the anger that bothers me. I see the hate triggered by the sight of our uniforms. What's with people and their attitudes against authority? When I was a kid, somebody in authority said jump and you said, how high?" lamented Butch.

"And you wonder why we've all started to greet each other with the phrase 'we're doomed'," added Big Jack without looking up from the stack of incident reports he was processing.

"What do you expect when budgets have been slashed and there's no more safety net?" observed Callahan.

"Here you go with your liberal spiel, throwing money at problems when we really need attitude adjustment, common decency, and good old fashioned respect," countered Ralph.

"With the safety net gone, inner-city kids have to fend for themselves. The gang is their new family," countered Callahan.

"You guys think those kids are badass. You know who really worries me?" asked Sammy.

"Who?" asked Big Jack who had watched Sammy grow from a mall rat to a thoughtful student well versed in worldly topics extending far beyond mall happenings.

"Pound for pound, these local douchebags are no match for the 'Lost Ones'," said Sammy.

"Who the hell are they?" asked Big Jack. "I'm buried in crime reports and hadn't heard about them."

"They're the young refugees. The diaspora that resulted from thirty years of conflict in hell hole places like Iraq, Afghanistan, and Syria. They're battle hardened. They've survived the atrocities of refugee camps, warlords, and famine," Sammy explained.

"Now wait a minute," cautioned Callahan. "You know that Hitler's Holocaust exterminated over six million Jews in the 1940s. There's no way of measuring how many millions of survivors suffered lifelong PTSD. Untold numbers were scarred physically and emotionally for life."

"What's that got to do with my Lost Ones?" asked Sammy.

"Well, the vast majority of Holocaust survivors pieced together a life, plodded on, and in many cases achieved the American dream. So why can't your Lost Ones do the same?"

"That was then. This is now. Everybody felt bad about the Holocaust survivors. That's how Israel got created. But we treat the Lost Ones like they're a virus to be avoided and contained. Kick 'em around long enough and they're gonna kick back," countered Sammy who had a habit of getting agitated when others struggled with connecting the dots.

"I guess you're right," said Callahan who could be cantankerous but deep down was more comfortable with compromise and opted for the long game in conversations. With elbows on the table and his head tilted to the left, supported by the palm of his hand, he wistfully commented, "Remember how everyone was bracing for Y2K mayhem back when 1999 turned to 2000. Turns out that the real mayhem was caused by human extremists, not computer glitches."

Everyone exhaled in acknowledgment. Lunch break was over and there were patrols to finish.

Mall cops adapted and so did Sammy. The transition was gradual but steady. They went from armed only with two-way radios to nightsticks and mace one year. Within two years, tasers were added. A couple of years later they were supplied with Glock semi-automatic pistols, full body armor, and body cameras. Each crop of new cops enthusiastically embraced the upgrades. However, deep down everyone, including veterans and rookies alike, knew the stakes were growing higher with each passing year.

Sammy evolved right along with the mall cops. These were the years he learned how to use both his wits and his fists. He knew when to face down an aggressor with the simple question, "You and whose army?" Likewise, he learned to not jump to conclusions and accuse the wrong person of a crime. He became as comfortable assembling a weapon as he was at interpreting a personality. Hanging around the mall cops, going on calls, and being privy to conversations about the state of world affairs was a real-life reality show that his classmates missed. There is only so much you can learn from textbooks and lectures. There is no substitute for a "ride-along-in-life".

Chapter 17:
Chameleons

For years Callahan rode solo in the mall security vehicle. He alternated between oldies' stations and insightful interviews on National Public Radio (NPR). Being paired with rookie Nicco opened doors to rooms that radio hosts only cracked open.

Callahan's go-to question for younger coworkers was, "So where did you grow up?"

"My dad moved from Puerto Rico by the time I started school. I guess you could say I was a prisoner of BellHaven schools," Nicco said with a nervous laugh.

"I've heard BellHaven schools suck," said Callahan with a casual air that masked a deeper interest in school systems. He had been certified to teach social studies many years ago but never had the opportunity to share his love of history.

"School was OK if you find the right crew, stick together, and don't take shit from anybody," said Nicco as he absentmindedly gazed across the vast parking lot extending toward the bus shelter.

"So what happens if your crew doesn't back you up?"

"Ever watch those animal shows when the old zebra falls behind the herd and the lions pick him off?"

"I see," said Callahan who added, "That's why we all come running when a ten-thirteen call goes out. Here we watch each other's backs. Too bad the rest of society doesn't."

"That's why I'm gonna be a cop. I'm joining the biggest badass gang and get paid for it," said Nicco with a mixture of confidence and youthful innocence.

With the mall closing for the night in a few minutes, it was time to move along a group of five youths lingering by the doorway just inside the food court. Nicco sauntered toward the black youngsters, the oldest of whom was no more than thirteen. With his nightstick swinging from his hip and his chest puffed out, he was in roust them mode. Maybe it was a Puerto Rican versus Black thing. Maybe it was payback for run-ins with their older brothers.

Whatever his motivation, Callahan responded with the disarming question, "So who's gonna win the Super Bowl?" The group consensus was that the New England Patriots were past their prime and the Atlanta Falcons would be flying high. Callahan let it be known that he didn't support any teams south of the Mason-Dixon line. This was met with blank stares so he offered a brief civil war lesson. Two of the five youngsters seemed mildly interested while the other three scornfully stared at what they thought was a crazy old white guy talking about ancient history. Sensing some interest and cerebral activity among two of the five, he posed the question, "What do you think about starting a NEW Underground Railroad?"

Only one of the two remaining listeners knew what the Underground Railroad was so he asked, "Why do we need a new one?"

Callahan jumped at the chance to float an idea that had been rolling around in his head. He asked, "How would you like a fresh start, a chance to start life in a better place?"

"Sure," said his solitary student, whose eyes shifted between Callahan and Nicco, not sure where this was going.

"Some kids want to break away from gangs but don't know how, right?"

"Yea," said the youngster who was now fishing in the pocket of his puffy jacket, searching for his phone.

"Well, a new Underground Railroad would be like the witness protection program. New life, new friends—and good friends, not the knuckleheads that hold you back," said Callahan with the enthusiasm of a preacher delivering a sermon.

"Mister, you might be right. I got to go. The bus is coming."

Callahan wasn't sure if he was just being polite and then smiled to himself thinking, just being polite is a good start.

Nicco asked Callahan, "Why bother being nice to them? They're dumb as dirt. You know they hate your guts and they don't give a shit about history?"

"Casual contact gets us intel. Also, who knows, maybe they'll realize we're human just like them. Might even break through to some numbnuts."

"This only works with really small groups. I don't know how teachers with big classes put up with them day in and day out. I'll be a cop any day over being a teacher. At least as a cop you can cuff 'em."

Callahan let that comment slide, knowing that time and experience would eventually either make Nicco or break him.

Sure enough, the next night on the eve of the Super Bowl, Nicco and Callahan contended with an extremely belligerent batch of over forty youths. Several of them were from the same group that he tried to chat nicely with the prior evening. Tonight they were jumping on tables, hooting, howling, and play fighting. Crowd control replaced the rapport building mode of Officer Friendly. Callahan even got into it with a local cop who commented, "Leave them alone, they're just kids."

Callahan kept his Irish temper in check and thought to himself, you take these kids home and try to get them off our property after negotiating with them for hours.

"Even the cops are running scared of these kids," quipped Nicco under his breath. "When I'm a cop, I'm not gonna take their crap."

"Just remember that one bad day and one bad incident and your cop career could be over, so watch your back and make sure you have a Plan B," advised Callahan as they stood by, allowing the crowd to disperse. When Callahan drifted off to sleep after this stressful shift, he had a strange dream about shape-shifting chameleons infiltrating, adapting, and surviving.

Chapter 18:
Coast Guard versus Marines

As senior year in high school approached, decisions had to be made. Where would Sammy go? Military academy was a logical choice given his smarts and athletic prowess. Under the tutelage of Uncles Butch and Ralph and a cadre of trainers from his extended family, Sammy mastered martial arts disciplines that included Krav Maga. Sammy's whole life was a boot camp, so he would be a natural leader once he arrived at a military academy.

It also made sense if Uncle Sam paid the bill.

As with so many important life decisions, debating the pros and cons took place in the back room of Willy's Water Hole.

Callahan kicked off the discussion proudly noting, "Sammy's speed on land places him first in the mile run and second place in the five-thousand yard swim. That's why they call him 'the Wolf', kicking ass in endurance events."

"Running and swimming from your enemy is fine but sometimes you got to stand your ground and fight," said ex-Marine Butch. Callahan laughed, fondly recalling the time Butch and Ralph gave Sammy some Krav Maga lessons so he could kick the asses of three bullies in middle school.

"Yea, I forgot about that," said Ralph, "wish I was there to see it."

"OK, so it's settled. After he graduates, off to Paris Island he goes," said Butch.

"Not so fast," said Callahan.

"What do you mean?" asked Butch. "See that Marine Corps flag over the bar? Sammy's the 'few' they refer to in the mantra 'a few good men'. Plus, the way the world's headed lately, we need more knights in armor like in the Middle Ages."

Callahan knew he was outnumbered. Still he persisted. "First of all," said Callahan, "he can sign up for a delayed entry program. Now they encourage kids entering the service to take a year off for real world experience so they're more mature when they enter."

"What'll he do during that year?" asked Butch who was getting increasingly impatient over what he called this 'delayed-entry bullshit'. "That's the problem with this country. Kids are not growing up. When do they get to be adults and wear their big boy pants?"

"So here's my plan," said Callahan in his juggernaut manner of speech. "He spends the year working officially as a mall cop since he'll be eighteen. After all these years shadowing us working in the background, which you guys know he wasn't supposed to be doing, he can officially become a mall cop."

"Lucky him," said Ralph sarcastically.

Callahan knew he had to score points so he quickly added, "Sammy will continue to spend weekends with you guys teaching him survival stuff like fishing, fighting, and living off the grid."

"Too bad every kid in America didn't get the training we've been giving to Sammy. There'd be a lot fewer snowflakes and nitwits," said Ralph.

"So it's decided, he goes into the military after we teach him everything we know. Now we just have to decide what branch," said Callahan.

"I thought we decided that: Marines, of course," said Butch.

"Well, Sammy takes to water like a fish and spends weekends during the summer with Uncle Joe, right?"

"Yea, what's Uncle Joe got to do with this?" said Butch who was getting impatient again.

Now Uncle Joe was not a mall cop, nor was he a real uncle to Sammy. His passion was sailing and he taught Sammy all things nautical. Callahan was no help in this regard. When he was at the helm, he would sink a boat within minutes. Furthermore, the slightest wave action would trigger projectile vomit.

"So are you thinking of the navy instead of the marines?" asked Ralph with an air of disappointment, while still being open minded since the marines are within the navy family.

"Well," said Callahan, pausing nervously. "I was thinking of the Coast Guard."

Deafening silence was followed by hooting and hollering.

Uncle Butch went so far as to offer to buy Sammy a nice sundress so he would have something to wear in that girly branch of the service.

"Listen," said Callahan, "the Coast Guard is America's first line of defense, right?"

"You got that right," said Butch. "Head 'em off at the pass like in the old cowboy movies except on the high seas. Cut the scoundrels off before they reach our coastlines."

"You all know that Sammy's interested in a career in law enforcement. So the Coast Guard will give him experience catching drug dealers, weapons traders, and even the sex trade scumbags," said Callahan.

"I read somewhere that pirates are making a comeback: one of them even goes by the name Black Beard, a friggin' knockoff," said Ralph.

"Swashbuckling fights with pirates and some terrorists mixed in for good measure," added Callahan who sensed he was getting the upper hand.

A few more rounds served on Callahan's tab and the vote for the Coast Guard was secured.

As Callahan exited Willy's Water Hole he stopped in his tracks. "I forgot one thing," he said.

"What's that?" said Butch, thinking he left his Kelly green Irish riding cap in the bar.

"We need to run this by Sammy," said Callahan, to which Butch said, "That would be nice, and let me know how it works out."

A few days after the debate, Callahan asked Sammy at dinner if he was considering the Coast Guard.

"Well," said Sammy. "I was actually considering specializing as a Marine sniper."

That's when Callahan paused, setting aside his stout, and asked, "Would you really want to put another human in your sites and snuff 'em out?" Sammy hesitated and before he could respond, Callahan added, "You realize that when you're captured they'll give you special treatment. This won't be like a video game where you can shut off the remote."

"You're right," admitted Sammy. "Plus, the Coast Guard could lead to a career in law enforcement."

"Yea, think of the Coast Guard as being mall cops on the high seas," said Callahan.

"I'm sure I can handle the physical stuff. I just don't know if I'll fit in."

"What do you mean? You'll do fine. What're you worried about? Hanging around the mall riding along with me and the guys was great training."

"Training for what?" asked Sammy.

"Whatever life throws at you. Think of all the characters you've met. The good, the bad, and the ugly."

"There certainly have been plenty of ugly."

"We've had our share of antics at the mall. You'll have your share of antics in the Coast Guard. I'll be waiting back here to hear all about 'em."

"You may be right. Hey, I got to get to the gym, see you later."

Once Sammy was safely out of earshot, Callahan shared a secret with Maggie. She was nearby, baking one of her famous apple pies. "You know the real reason I'm glad he's joining the Coast Guard?"

"Why, is it because it's just up the road in New London?"

"Well, that's one reason. But the real reason is because they don't get killed like in the army and marines. They're usually not on the front lines when all hell breaks loose."

"I'm not comfortable having him in any branch of the service in these crazy times," said Maggie with a mother's frown. "Have you noticed that anybody in a uniform, whether here in the States or overseas, has a target on their back? God only knows where they'll send him. Hasn't it occurred to you that we're at war with just about everyone and everywhere? And who's the enemy? I've lost track."

"That's my point. The Coast Guard isn't sent to the hottest spots," said Callahan as he leaned forward, clasping his hands together as if offering up a prayer. "I do worry that the navy might take them over if the shit hits the fan. Oh well, everybody loves the Coast Guard. They rescue people. Their mission's clear."

At this point Callahan wasn't sure if he was talking to himself or if he still had an audience with Maggie. "Speaking of joining the service, do you think I should sign up for something?" ventured Callahan with a devilish grin.

"What the hell are you talking about?" said Maggie without looking up from trimming the pie crust.

"All I'm saying is there should be a place for a guy like me. I just want three hots and a cot for the balance of my life. Is that too much to ask for?"

"That's the problem with you. You're so negative. Can't you aim higher?"

"If I wanted to aim high, maybe I should have joined the air force. Isn't that their motto? Anyways, that's the problem with you. Always thinking some pot of gold is going to appear. Well, it's not. The bills keep piling up while we keep going down. I got Parent PLUS student loans that'll last till I'm ninety. Why can't I just coast out? Do you have any idea how tired I am?"

"Just help me set the table for dessert," said Maggie as she placed the pie in the center of the table.

Callahan shoved aside junk that perpetually cluttered the kitchen table, tossing plates in the general vicinity of where they should be. Slinking off to his computer, he muttered to himself, "She's worried about dessert, I'm worried about our existence."

Chapter 19:
Brothers

Sammy was running late for his reunion with members of Callahan & Company at Willy's Water Hole. It was the Wednesday before Thursday Thanksgiving. Traffic coming back from the Coast Guard Academy was heavy. That's why Sammy had not changed from his Coast Guard blues. He was not one to flaunt his military service. He was not an ostentatious guy. Beyond personal modesty, there were practical safety related reasons. Members of armed forces had been frequent targets of attack from the disenfranchised of the far right and the far left.

Both Anarchists and Aliens viewed the military as oppressors whose sole role was to keep the masses in line.

Far right militia groups called themselves Patriot Pride. They felt the government wimped out and didn't do enough to tamp down the radical leftie subversives. They considered themselves the last line of defense in America's moral war.

Far left militia groups included the disaffected, the have-nots, the aliens, and many of the Lost Ones. They

felt the government abandoned them and their only re-
course was to take back what was owed to them. Take
backs included land, reparations, citizenship, student
loans, Social Security, and health insurance. They had
been radicalized by the Great Compromise that followed
the post-9/11 era.

Far right and far left had one thing in common. Hate
it all. Clean the slate. Somehow start from scratch.

As Sammy entered the bar, he was saluted by Willy,
the burly, bearded owner-bartender. Willy saw action in
the house-to-house fighting in Fallujah during the US
surge to retain Iraq. Willy lost some buddies in that campaign so he was quick to offer support and
acknowledgment to fellow servicemen.

This acknowledgment incensed the two members of
the Black Panthers who had recently adopted Willy's
Water Hole to expand their outreach. This bar is located
in what's considered borderland. The northern section
of urban BellHaven butts up against the aging southern
section of Northville. It's the mixing pot for disillusioned
suburbanites with the demoralized city dwellers.

"What's up, Tom?" snarled a Panther in his black
leather jacket as he leaned forward from the corner table.
Beneath his black beret, the Panther's contemptuous
stare sized up this brother in navy blue BDUs.

"The name's Sammy, and I'm fine," Sammy curtly replied.

The second Panther, peering from behind sunglasses under a black baseball cap, asked, "You fine with steppin' for the man?"

"Listen, I paid my dues and learned a shitload of stuff, all on Uncle Sam's dime," retorted Sammy.

"Yea, the same Uncle Sam that forced Indians from Georgia to Oklahoma on the Trail of Tears. You see, I may look black but I'm half Indian and I don't forget"

"Hey, we got something in common. I look black but I'm half Korean," said Sammy.

"I knew there was something different about you, Tom, I mean, Sam."

"So I get doubly screwed. I get pulled over for Driving While Black and I got no country to call home. The Korean peninsula is now a nuclear toxic crater."

"The USA really did a number on you" said Mr. Black Cap. This biracial connection caused him to ease up slightly on the pedal of animosity.

The Panther in the black leather jacket and black beret remained caustic. This talk of cross-cultures struck a nerve with him. He was an all-American African American. "Well, let me tell you my history, my brother.

"I was raised by a single mom. She did everything she could until beatings by my old man forced us into shelters. She was just getting back on her feet, moving up from being a CNA cleaning bedpans to a full nurse when, guess what?"

"What?" said Sammy, knowing the importance of showing empathy and practicing active listening.

"They took away the scholarships. Why? Because Uncle Sam had to fund the war machine. She tried to keep working three jobs but it finally killed her. Cause of death: Uncle Sam.

"So let me ask you, Coast Guard boy, why don't you take that shit they taught you and help us stand up to the man?"

Sammy bristled but his wits took charge of his fists. "First of all, let's skip the 'boy' talk. You, of all people, should know that boy reference gets us nowhere. As for your deadbeat dad, I'm sorry for that. I had no dad. Mom got pregnant and he was gone. End of story. In fact, she abandoned me in a bathroom at the mall."

Both Panthers were at a rare loss for words absorbing Sammy's story.

"So you know what saved me?" said Sammy. "I was raised by wolves."

"Get out, you were raised in the woods?" both Panthers said in unison.

"Not quite, but a bunch of people who behave like wolves, travel in packs, and fight to defend themselves made me a part of their pack."

"I could have used a pack like that," said the angry Panther, whose stare went way past Sammy to a distant, painful childhood.

"Maybe the Panthers can be your pack. All this talk of wolves and panthers, it's turning into a friggin' jungle," said Sammy. And with that lighter comment, they agreed to disagree, but the seed had been planted and a rumble averted. Fists didn't fly but there would be no bro-hugs tonight. Breaths become shallow and the air hangs heavy when the doors to each other's lives swing wide open.

As Sammy moseyed down the bar to join the cop hairs of his adopted, extended family, black jacket, black beret Panther said under his breath, "Pawn of the state and friend of the enemy."

Panther in the black baseball cap and sunglasses just scanned the crowd, finally commenting, "We all got history, let's get outta here."

The gathering of Callahan & Company was larger tonight because of Thanksgiving Eve. Willy's Water Hole was an eclectic mix of characters tonight. Corporal Wheeler from the mall force was now Captain Wheeler of the US Army. He just returned from his tour of duty trying to win the hearts and minds of villagers in far-flung godforsaken places. He made a career of military service and shipped out to Africa on his first tour of duty not long after he and Callahan found Sammy on the bathroom floor. This was a special reunion. He kept saying to Sammy, "Wow look at how big you got!" to which Sammy replied, "I would hope so."

Wheeler had plenty of stories to tell but the questions he avoided answering were:

Are you married?

Who are you seeing?

When are you gonna retire from the army?

As with most guys, he was quick to discuss sports and politics. But with personal stuff the policy was don't ask, don't tell. Mall cop stories were shared and Wheeler was brought up to speed on mall gossip. He said, "Knuckleheads need to spend a year on the Nile to appreciate how bad life can be. Here in the States, we had the Great

Crash and the Great Compromise, but cops still come when called. In other places, there's no cops, just the biggest, baddest warlord."

Junior perked up hearing the word warlord exclaiming, "That may not be so bad, at least over there justice is swift."

Wheeler cautioned him saying, "Over there the justice depends upon which end of the stick you're at."

Wheeler spent most of his military career in Africa trying to build communities in the image and likeness of the USA. Since Sammy's Coast Guard duties were limited to ports of call, he was intrigued by Wheeler's African experience deep in the hinterland. Wheeler's response was like that of a doctor breaking the news to a family whose patient is terminally ill. Sammy was doubly disappointed since he always harbored the dream of touring both his African and Korean roots. The former was now too dangerous to visit and the latter was decimated.

Reunions can be tricky. Times change. Hearts harden. Connections severed.

Not so for Callahan & Company.

Though they hailed from different ages and cultures, the need to ban together was never greater. Nothing stimulates unity better than adversity.

Mingling at bars over a pitcher of beer and camaraderie on a pickup game of basketball were becoming a rarity. Callahan & Company knew it was time to close ranks as militia of all stripes began frequenting both Burpee's Diner and Willy's Water Hole. By the end of the evening and after a few rounds, discussions turned to buying a bar where politics, animosity, and guns could be checked at the door, just like you check your coat in the coat closet. Suggested bar names included Sammy's Saloon and Callahan's Corner.

Big Jack was holding court along the back wall of the bar when he spotted Callahan hobnobbing among the crowd. Callahan corralled glassy eyed patrons announcing, "We need to form 'The Legion'."

Younger patrons offered polite, blank stares masking thoughts that, maybe this guy was in early stages of Alzheimers. Others, who were more juiced up on alcohol, picked up on his proposal. Alcohol has a way of triggering deeper thoughts, at least in the opinion of the drinker.

Sensing an audience, Callahan continued, "We need a new version of the French Foreign Legion."

Captain Wheeler was immediately on board with this romantic vision of the French Foreign Legion battling Algerian rebels. He shouted over the din of the bar crowd, "Remember that show *Rat Patrol* with jeeps mounted with fifty caliber machine guns doing donuts kicking up sand in the desert."

As the jukebox blared the song "The Boys Are Back in Town" by Tin Lizzy, Callahan shouted, "It could be like the Peace Corps on steroids. Only go into countries where we have a chance of success."

"So your Legion is not gonna chase these rebel rats across the North African desert?" asked Wheeler.

"Sorry, Wheeler," said Callahan, "my Legion does stuff like build roads, dig wells, plant trees, you know all that go-green stuff. Don't get me wrong, they're trained, armed, and ready to defend themselves to kick as much ass as they need to."

"Ahh," said Wheeler. "That's the Callahan I remember. I thought for a minute you became some sort of namby-pamby tree-hugging liberal."

Sammy jumped in asking, "How about having the Coast Guard be the Foreign Legion on the high seas? We need protection once we leave the USA."

"Wait a minute," said Wheeler, "are we talking about protecting every US ship of every size? How about the big shots on their yachts?"

Callahan responded without skipping a beat. "If they're rich enough to have a yacht, they can defend themselves. They can hire their own security."

Wheeler leaned forward slightly, spilling his beer, while giving a quick look around to see who might be listening, "So your Foreign Legion would be like Marines protecting the US embassies in Iran during the Iranian hostage crisis and repulsing Al Qaeda in Benghazi."

The trio went silent in the midst of this raucous bar as the last chorus of "The Boys Are Back in Town" melded into the Clash rendition of "Should I Stay or Should I Go."

Callahan broke the silence proclaiming, "This is exactly why we should only go where we succeed." And with that, he shouted, "Check out the words of the song, that's what I'm talking about."

By the time Callahan crawled to the back wall of the bar with stout in hand, he joined up with Big Jack who was carousing with Uncles Ralph and Butch. As usual whenever mall cops gather, they recount interactions with assholes. The shoplifters that mumble, the fighters that spit, the privileged that think their shit don't stink, and the underprivileged that think everybody owes them something. Within this backdrop, Callahan continued to pedal his Domestic Foreign Legion.

Big Jack raised his eyebrows asking, "How can it be domestic if it's a Foreign Legion?"

"Shut up, it's the liquor talking, we'll figure out a name later," said Callahan.

Ralph lamented about shoplifters, saying, "They dress well. It's not like they're running around naked in the cold. They're well fed, in fact half of them are fat." Callahan was still rethinking a name for his Foreign Legion.

Oblivious to Ralph's rant, Callahan carved the word "Legion" into the dark oak wood table among carvings that professed undying love to one-time sweethearts.

"They steal because they can, it's as simple as that," offered Butch. "The other group I worry about are the junkies. Skins pasty and movements jerky. I feel sorry for them until they fight."

"What the teens and junkies have in common is a need for attitude adjustment," said Callahan, waving his pen knife. "Their moral compass needs to be reset. They've been acting that way for years. Maybe a couple of years in isolation will do 'em some good."

"So what are you suggesting, Mr. Philosopher?" asked Ralph.

"I'm saying if they joined my Domestic Legion or whatever the hell we call it, they could spend a couple of years adjusting their attitudes, resetting their compass, and contributing to society."

"I'm no flaming liberal but this is sounding like brainwashing. It's got a red China sound to it," said Butch.

"These mutts have been acting like knuckleheads for so long, they don't know anything else. They need attitude adjustment, behavior modification. A complete break from their idiot friends. If that's re-educating or brainwashing, then so be it," said Callahan.

Once Callahan was revved up on a topic, it was hard to reel him back. Fortunately Ralph, ever the hungry pragmatist, redirected the conversation with an order of onion rings.

Chapter 20:
Hiccups at Burpee's

Sammy tied his hybrid bike to the no parking sign outside Burpee's Diner. Hybrids with fatter tires were ideal for navigating the sidewalks of Northville where they existed and the sidewalks of BellHaven where they had not yet crumbled. Biking was Sammy's escape from reality while keeping in shape during his brief but pleasant visits to Callahan. Attending Oxford on a Rhodes Scholarship afforded the opportunity to bike the rolling hills of England when not immersed in studies. Spending time on the "other side of the pond" gave Sammy an out-of-country experience akin to an out-of-body experience.

A convoy of cop cars with sirens blaring zoomed northward on Main Street. Sammy suspected they were enroute to the mall, especially when they included the K-9 units.

Sammy headed for the corner booth where he customarily met members of Callahan & Company. Today he was meeting Uncles Butch and Ralph.

"I hope they don't get caught up in the mall mess," thought Sammy. Sure enough, they were running late because of a skirmish between groups known as Anarchists and Aliens.

Their names reflected their origins.

The Anarchists

They were youths who gave up on the American dream. They lost any reason to respect authority. They were the children of service workers and factory workers. They were the children of those downsized by automation. They were predominantly from white, lower income families but their membership swelled when middle class cohorts saddled with enormous college debt could not find work. They spent their free time bucking the system, or fucking the system, as they preferred to call it. Fighting, bartering, and living off the grid made more sense to them than playing nice on the grid.

The Aliens

They were primarily Latino youth whose families were uprooted by the deportations of the last ten years. When the Great Crash shocked the economy, they were the last on the economic boat and the first kicked overboard. Such was the plight of the Aliens, who like the Anarchists had given up on the American dream. Although predominantly Latino, their membership included loose alliances with displaced youth and refugees from all cultures. As with the Anarchists, they found no reason to play nice on the grid.

Although they shared common barriers and circumstances, the Anarchists and the Aliens battled each other rather than direct their wrath at the powers that be.

Sammy sidestepped the usual seating area since it was occupied by two burly, middle-aged, balding white guys and a skinny teen with a black baseball cap pulled low on his forehead. All three were wearing plaid flannel shirts and camouflage pants. Sammy glanced from under his black hoodie just long enough to catch the ire of these red-blooded patriots. Back in the day, one of them would have asked him, "What are you looking at, boy?" Years of attempted civil rights and political correctness elicited the more subtle but snide comment, "Better lock up the silverware." Sammy didn't have to read lips knowing he wasn't welcome in that corner.

Being within earshot of the silverware comment, Sammy had a flashback to the three thugs who bullied him in the schoolyard of middle school. He smiled and recalled kicking their asses in quick order. Ah, the good old days, thought Sammy. Maybe a retort like, "What are you looking at?" would teach these corner cretins a lesson. But then again, these old dogs were not about to learn any new tricks, thought Sammy. He was streetwise enough to know there were Berettas holstered under those flannel shirts.

Sammy ordered a hearty dish of bacon, scrambled eggs, and home fries from the all-day-breakfast menu as he remained under surveillance. When his dish arrived, so did Uncles Butch and Ralph.

Ralph was the first to confirm that, "Assholes were fighting again at the mall."

"Was it the Aliens or the Anarchists?" asked Sammy.

"I don't know and don't care," scoffed Butch, "They're all assholes. We got lucky. Shift ended. We were already headed this way."

"Yea," added Ralph. "Plus the cops handle everything now. We're just chicken shit, all we do is observe and report. In fact, even the cops don't do shit. Scared of their own shadows. Afraid of lawsuits. I wonder if they just stand by waiting for the herd to thin itself out."

"Would that be such a bad thing?" said Ralph.

When Butch and Ralph entered the diner, they offered the ceremonial nod of acknowledgment to their compadres in the corner. They played ball on the same teams back in the school days. Times and circumstances had changed for Butch and Ralph but not so for their former classmates. No words were exchanged but these old-school associates were incensed at the sight of Butch and Ralph sitting with this young punk. For them it was more evidence that society was in a tailspin.

"Your camo friends in the corner have been giving you the stink eye," said Butch, being careful to limit eye contact.

"Too bad they don't know they're in the presence of an Oxford University graduate with degrees in international relations and economics," said Ralph who offered compliments sparingly and honestly.

"I'm in the home stretch to graduate. But you know something, it wouldn't make much difference to them. I could be master of the universe and I'm still a local punk to them," shrugged Sammy.

"So how's it going in England?" asked Butch as he ordered a Philly Cheesesteak without glancing at the menu. "I thought you were aiming for a law enforcement career. What happened to the mall cop, Coast Guard, enforcer-turned-FBI agent? I figured you'd become a prosecutor and end up on the supreme court?"

"Traveling to ports with the Coast Guard gave me the international bug," said Sammy. "Palling around with you guys and the mall's cleaning crew exposed me to the world. Dealing with knuckleheads made me appreciate the art of negotiation."

"So are you thinking about joining the State Department as a Foreign Service Officer or are you gonna be the next James Bond?" chuckled Ralph.

"Well," said Sammy, leaning back in the booth, pushing the last of his home fries to the corner of his plate, "they are looking to diversify the 007 image and maybe an Afro-Asian guy would fit the bill."

"Let me know when that premiers and save me a front row seat," laughed Butch.

"Even secret agents got to pee, I'll be right back," said Sammy.

Ralph made a head nod toward the corner, quietly commenting, "That used to be me not so long ago."

"Me too," said Butch, "I was a hard core redneck back in the day. Remember the good old days when we ran the neighborhood and kicked intruders' asses."

"Sammy's arrival changed all that," said Ralph.

"Actually I started changing before he was born," said Butch.

"If you did, you kept it secret," said Ralph, stroking his mustache and making that rare eye to eye contact when guys talk about something more serious.

"Marge and I never had kids. Probably just as well. Can't raise a kid on a mall cop's salary," said Butch.

"You know that's right. I worked three jobs at the same time, one for each kid."

"The pictures of dead refugee kids washing up on the shores of the Mediterranean started getting to me. Got me to thinking, if we adopted one, we might just save one."

"So where did Sammy come in?"

"Marge and I never could pull ourselves to adopt. Just couldn't take that leap. Plus we couldn't afford it. With Sammy, we could help as part of a bigger team. Sort of adoption on the cheap."

"Strength in numbers. Spread the blame in case we didn't get it right with Sammy," said Ralph, stirring coffee that didn't really need stirring.

"Well we got it right with him," said Butch.

"How much of this was Sammy and how much of this was us?"

"Little bit of both. He needed us and we needed him."

"Just like he needed us today to face down those redneck assholes," said Ralph, keeping one eye on his former friends.

"Yea, takes an asshole to know an asshole," said Butch.

"Who are you calling an asshole, me or them?" shot back Ralph.

"Shut up and pay up and let's get out of here," said Butch, inching his way out of the booth. "Next time we sit at a table so my fat ass doesn't get stuck."

On that note, Sammy returned from the bathroom, gathered his backpack. "I got to check on Callahan. On my last call to him, he was rambling on about booby trapping the lawn to deter marauders."

"That sounds like Callahan," chucked Butch.

Sammy said Callahan's son Bryce was working on a new version of silly string for the military that when disturbed would trigger an alarm announcing intruders.

"Imagine that, high tech and Callahan still grabs his shotgun to finish them off, welcome to the new America," laughed Butch.

"Hey, before we leave there's something you should know about the booth in the other corner," said Ralph with a hushed nervousness on the cusp of a touchy-feely topic.

"What about it?" said Sammy as he almost forgot to pick up his bike helmet from under the table. "Is it haunted or something?"

"It's a good haunting. It's where we met years ago when you were only a few weeks old. That's where we came up with your name," said Ralph.

"I never heard the full story and never really thought about it much. You guys always kept me too busy to dwell on the past," said Sammy with alternating glances at Butch and Ralph, not sure if he wanted the full story.

"Back then there were these jukeboxes at each booth," explained Butch.

"What the hells a jukebox?" asked Sammy.

"Think of an iPod in a giant glass case and you have to put money in it to hear a song," said Butch.

"Sounds like the Middle Ages," laughed Sammy.

"Anyways, this song is being sung by a guy named Sammy Davis and Callahan gets the bright idea to name you after him," said Butch.

"How liquored up were you guys?" asked Sammy.

"We were stone cold sober. It was lunchtime and we had our reasons," interjected Ralph.

"I always thought my real dad might have been named Sammy Davis. Deep down I always wondered why my last name never was Callahan," said Sammy. "There's moments when I think about my real dad but then I get right back to being me."

"We don't give him much thought either. Whereabouts unknown and probably not good," said Ralph, waving his hand as if swatting a pesky fly.

"You just keep being you, push on like the rest of us, and don't be weighed down by the past," Butch nervously added.

"Callahan never adopted you but instead was your official guardian. That was part of the deal. He agreed to do this but only if the rest of us signed up to help. We're the backup team," explained Ralph.

The three men stood by the booth, staring down upon empty plates waiting to be washed and a tip waiting to be picked up. They proceeded toward the diner exit, following that silent cue all guys follow when enough's been said. Enroute to the door and passing the cashier, the uncles masked the stiffness of their knees in the presence of their former teammates.

Butch and Ralph saluted these ex-friends, giving the impression they had to be somewhere in a hurry. Once in the parking lot, Butch noted to Ralph that seeing them was like old water cascading over a crumbling bridge. Ralph agreed saying, "We no longer play on the same team," and "check out how they're training a new asshole."

Chapter 21:
Red versus Blue...
Maroon and Yellow Get a Vote Too

As time went by, conversations about the OTHERS took on an urgency among members of Callahan & Company. Verbal matches in the kitchen and talking heads on TV became more important than speaking the truth. Callahan got fed up and issued the following edict, "You know how nightclubs frisk patrons and ban guns so everyone stays safe and enjoys themselves?"

Sammy said, "Yea, so what's that got to do with us?"

"Well at this table, no verbal guns are allowed. Everybody needs to take their turn speaking. Better yet, everybody needs to take turns listening. This means not just running your mouth. You have to listen to each other."

Sammy winked to Uncles Ralph and Butch, since they knew what was coming next.

"Anybody who says anything absolutely false must be rejected," said Callahan, slamming a fork on the table like a judge's gavel.

"Thank God Junior and his conspiracy theories are not at the table tonight," laughed Kevin.

Sammy seized the opportunity to practice debating skills. "So what makes something be the truth? Black and white is easy but what about the grays?" Silence followed. For this, there was no quick answer.

Callahan picked absentmindedly with his fork at Santa's face on a faded place mat. Christmas themed decorations had a way of never getting put away in the Callahan household. The Christmas spirit was long gone but nobody had the time or energy to put the tchotchke away. Conversational uncertainty was broken when Callahan made the following observation, "A person's essence can be detected by their bumper stickers, their car, their appearance. I remember when the biggest rivalry was the Red Socks versus the Yankees or the Giants versus the Patriots. Now, nobody cares about your favorite team. It's all about what tribe you belong to."

"Yea," agreed Kevin, who just returned from D.C. having spoken at a conference dealing with the question of presenting news without supporting any particular faction. Kevin lamented, "Wearing a shirt or slapping on a bumper sticker invites scorn. It goes way beyond political differences. Value judgments are heaped onto stereotypes like gravy on mashed potatoes."

"I'm as patriotic as the next guy," said Butch. "I logged my time in Afghanistan. But I'm getting tired of these toy soldiers riding around waving guns and the red, white, and blue."

"Hey, Butch, you know what we need?" said Ralph, as he opened up a can of sardines along with a conversational can of worms.

"How can you eat that stuff? It stinks up the kitchen," said Butch.

"Doctor says fish oil's good for my cholesterol. Plus, I like the way the little fishies are lined up in the can, like the bullets in the clip of my Glock. Anyways, we need to add maroon to the red, white, and blue of Old Glory. Maybe we should put a maroon border around the flag."

"And I suppose I'm playing the role of Dolly Madison sewing this new flag for you," said Maggie as she crammed the last dish into an overstuffed cabinet. "You guys plan the world, I'm shuffling off to bed," she said as she maneuvered her walker down the narrow hallway to the bedroom.

"She's been going to bed earlier ever since I returned from Oxford for the holidays," said Sammy, hoping to elicit a reaction from this band of not-so-merry men.

They were absorbed with the issue of red versus blue with maroon to the rescue.

Ralph continued to make his case for maroon. "Look guys, it's a mix of red and blue. It could be a symbol of compromise and cooperation. That's why we have to make it the new border for Old Glory. Everything on the flag stands for something. The fifty stars are the states. The thirteen stripes are the original colonies. The maroon border could be the wraparound. You know, all for one and one for all, just like us."

"I'm with you on this except for one thing," said Butch. "You and I have been around long enough to know that when you keep giving in, after a while you give everything away. Maroon loses its identity. The reds think it's red. The blues think it's blue. In the end it becomes nothing. Maroon becomes a moron that neither side can trust."

This was Captain Wheeler's cue to offer a historic perspective. He happened to be on the state side for the holidays in between tours of duty in Africa.

"So, Butch, sounds like maroon would be like Neville Chamberlain caving in to Hitler, thinking he was preventing him from carving up Europe."

"Yea, mister international scholar, that's what I'm trying to say," said Butch.

"We're all sort of maroons," mused Callahan whose eyelids were getting heavy but his mind was still racing. "If you ask me, the maroons are like squirrels. They run left, they run right, they scamper around using a lot of energy. They don't accomplish anything and in the end everybody hates them anyway.

"There's only a few brownies left, finish 'em up and wash 'em down with a beer," coaxed Callahan, filling the momentary silence.

"How about a second border on the flag with the color yellow," offered Sammy, breaking the silence and testing his negotiation skills. "A rich dark maroon next to a bright yellow. Now that's a good combination."

"I'm no fan of yellow," said Ralph. "Chickens are that color. You want the USA to be known as a chicken? Haven't you heard the term you're nothin' but a yellow-bellied coward?"

Sammy prodded, "Why do parents expecting a baby pick yellow for the nursery?"

"Sometimes they don't know if it's gonna be a boy or girl. Sometimes they don't wanna know if it's a boy or girl. Maybe they're not stereotyping blue for boys and pink for girls," said Ralph. "What the hell's this baby color talk got to do with anything?"

"You just proved my point," said Sammy. "Yellow's the perfect color for people who either have no opinion or those who hide their opinion."

"Well that's the problem with these people," countered Ralph. "They're either too dumb to have an opinion or they're too sneaky to reveal their position. Either way, I have no use for 'em.

"And you know something else," said Ralph who was now on a roll, "I call the dumb ones the ostriches. Like an ostrich, they bury their heads in music, movies, games, and parties. I call the sneaky ones yellow snakes. They slither around and keep their loyalties to themselves. You never know if they're friend or foe."

"Enough about colors and animals. Leave the flag alone. It's not gonna change unless there's a civil war," sighed Callahan.

"That may be on the horizon," said Captain Wheeler in a hushed voice that a parent uses when discussing divorce in the presence of children. "I've been in Africa viewing the USA from afar. From where I sit, we look like a ship that's taking on water and starting to break up. Since I've been back, I've been talking to people, all sorts of people, and I don't like what I hear."

"So what are you hearing?" asked Sammy who enjoyed comparing his Coast Guard tours and his Oxford University experiences with Wheeler's third-world travels.

"Well, you know how we're always claiming to be exceptional and expect the rest of the world to catch up with us?" said Wheeler.

"Don't tell me the Africans are closing in on us!" said Butch.

"It's actually the opposite," said Wheeler. "We're getting more like them. I'm talking about tribal fighting and living hand-to-mouth, day-to-day. Over there, you get sick, you die, and the kids are orphaned. Guess what, it's happening here."

"We still got health insurance. You still can choose your doctor. The ambulance and cops still come when you call 'em," said Butch.

"What good is health insurance if you can't afford it?" countered Wheeler. "Skyrocketing costs and high deductibles. Take that ambulance ride and they may as well bring you to the poorhouse. Cops still show up but have you noticed that nobody wants to be a cop anymore? Who wants to work where you're damned if you do and damned if you don't?" said Wheeler, waving his knife as he picked at the burned remnants of the last brownie clinging to the edge of the aluminum pan.

"I have no problem questioning bad cops or even bad mall cops. We've had some losers over the years that washed out of our system. Good riddance," said Callahan.

"I'm just sayin', you guys are thinking everything's OK, but a murder here and a murder there and before you know it, we're living in warlord world. No cops, no rules. Actually, let me correct that. The rule is, I got the gun and the rest of you can kiss my ass," said Wheeler.

"I know what you mean," said Sammy, "but I've been to Puerto Rico with the Coast Guard helping out after a hurricane. They're dirt poor but they pull together. They're survivors. They work together."

"Exactly my point," said Wheeler. "We have less problems here but we still can't agree. Hell, even the pandemic didn't pull us together. Have you noticed how families have been disappearing when one parent dies? Where are they now? Safety net, what safety net?"

"You guys are all talking about big picture stuff. I only know what I know. Did you know that my mother and her three brothers were orphans?" said Callahan.

"We know, we know, it's the Christmas Story of the Callahan household," said Sammy, immediately remorseful that he might be sounding disrespectful and ungrateful.

"Yea, well it bears retelling," said Callahan. "My mom and her brothers all turned out OK thanks to their Aunt Kate who took them in. Raised them with tough love. Something that's in short supply nowadays. And that's why I keep reminding you guys."

"Kind of like the way you guys took me in," nodded Sammy.

With this affirmation, members of the kitchen cabinet instinctively sipped their beers like guys at a wedding who bolt for the bar when the music starts, fearing they might be asked to dance. Sammy's connecting this dot was about as warm and fuzzy as it gets in Callahan's world.

Sammy again floated the observation "Maggie was slowing down and amputations appeared inevitable."

This time he had an ally in Kevin who said, "I had been traveling and noticed the changes upon my return."

Cradling his chin in both hands and speaking to no one in particular, Callahan responded, "I've told her she's working herself into an early grave, but does she listen to me?. No! She's falling apart. This goddamn place is falling apart faster than I can fix it."

"Let's get ahead of the curve," said Kevin. "We could make the bathroom handicap accessible, install a ramp to the front door, convert the living room into her bedroom, complete with a hospital bed."

"Lots of good ideas, smart guy, but who's gonna pay for all this and who's gonna do it?" mumbled Callahan.

Captain Wheeler jumped in with his usual out-of-the-box suggestion. "You know how the Amish people build barns over a weekend?"

"Yea, what are we gonna do, hire some Amish workers?" said Butch.

"No, we could be the Amish," said Wheeler. "Think about it. We know enough guys with carpentry and electrical skills."

Butch started coming on board with this self-help notion. "We've already been gardening in summer and canning for winter. Why not join forces on the inside. We're already in survival mode so let's take it the next step," said Butch with increasing enthusiasm.

"We could even get Junior to help mix the cement. We could tell him we're building a wall to prevent an alien invasion," joked Ralph.

"While we're renovating, how about we reinforce Fort Callahan?" asked Callahan. "I always wanted to install those hurricane shutters like they have down south."

"This is New England, when was the last time we had a decent hurricane?" countered Ralph.

"I'm talking about hurricane shutters on the inside of the windows. They could work like the metal grates that get pulled down in front of stores when they close. Do you guys realize that windows are the weak spots for invasions? Just look at that picture window in the living room. Toss a brick and you're in," said Callahan.

"And who's gonna be tossing bricks to break into this dump?" asked Kevin who had moved out some years ago but always lamented that his childhood home could never be repaired, no matter how many shifts Callahan and Maggie worked.

"When darkness falls the off-road bikers swarm in from BellHaven. They rev up their motors at twilight. They don't give a shit about anything or anyone. They got nothing to lose. Every night hundreds of them looking for trouble and stealing anything that's not nailed down. Cops can't do anything. You, Sammy, and Wheeler have been globetrotting. You don't know how bad it's gotten around here," said Callahan.

"How about we insulate the hurricane shutters so you save on energy costs. From the street, the house will still look like a house, not a bunker. The building inspector doesn't need to know what's going on inside and the criminal element will be in for a surprise," offered Wheeler who wanted to elevate the conversation beyond Callahan's medieval castle concept. "We could even convert the fireplace to a wood burning stove so you have a secondary heat source in case all hell breaks loose."

"Finally you guys understand that Armageddon's just around the corner," exclaimed Callahan, waving his hands in the air like a trial lawyer making his final statement.

"So it's decided," said Sammy and Kevin, raising their glasses in a toast. "We all regroup next weekend to begin the renovations."

Like the knights of the round table, Callahan's kitchen cabinet pledged to return for as many weekends as it takes with muscle and material to see this project to conclusion. As the kitchen meeting adjourned, Callahan wryly asked, "So what am I supposed to be doing while you worker bees scurry about?"

Sammy patted him on the back saying, "You can supervise from your lounge chair with a beer in hand watching your beloved Patriots lose another game."

Sammy and his adopted siblings were keenly aware they were not rich. However, they knew there would always be food on the table and a roof over their heads. They grew up seeing every member of Callahan & Company working multiple jobs, getting gigs in the underground economy. There were singers, fixers, trainers, writers, and drivers just to name a few. If you had a skill, you could make a buck and share your expertise. No cash, no problem, there was always bartering. Just as important as making money, the barter economy nurtured a collective sense of survival and independence in the face of outside forces. While nuclear families and fractured families all too often fell prey to the vagaries of outside forces, Callahan & Company was adept at weathering such storms. This was most evident when Maggie's health deteriorated to the point at which her left leg was amputated. The following year, her right leg was amputated. Living in a ranch facilitated handicapped access but a ramp had to be built to get over the two front steps leading to the front door. The door to the bathroom had to be expanded to enable wheelchair access. A roll-in shower had to be installed to replace the tub. The living room to the left of the front door had to be retrofitted to a bedroom for Maggie, complete with a hospital bed. Meals had to be prepared for Maggie since she was no longer able to navigate the kitchen. This was the most discouraging since cooking was her passion and the kitchen was her domain.

Callahan was in no condition physically or financially to do all this retrofitting. Team effort by Callahan & Company made it a reality. Sammy and his siblings experienced firsthand what collective compassion can accomplish. Maggie was only able to enjoy these improvements a couple of years. Enjoy was an overly optimistic word given her deteriorated and painful condition. However, her final days were spent in the place she called home with the people she loved most.

After her passing, the support network remained in place for Callahan. In most other families, when the funeral ends, the guests drift away. The calls and visits to "touch base" to see how the bereaved are doing become fewer and farther between. The abundance of food and flowers at the height of the funeral become a distant memory. Not so for Callahan & Company post-funeral life.

Callahan was given time and space to grieve. Much of this was occupied by working his body in the gym and his mind in the library. His three-job work routine continued since bills had to be paid. Callahan was given his space but the extended family never allowed him to become untethered as so often happens with widows and widowers. This enabled him to keep one foot grounded in reality.

As for the other foot, that was a different matter. Long before Maggie's illness took its toll and eventually her life, Callahan was losing grip. The supports were always in place but he saw the handwriting on the wall. He had a gnawing sense of his own extinction. A way of life that was slipping away. A carefree childhood that could never be recaptured. Most alarming was the notion that he could not bring himself to wish marriage and children for Sammy and his own kids. For Callahan, life had become too hard, too complicated, and too fractured. The thought of starting life all over again as a newborn was too daunting. The thought of finding a soulmate for a lifetime relationship in uncertain times weighed heavy on his mind. His own pilot light was dimming and he feared that his malaise might become contagious.

Chapter 22:
Auld Lang Syne

Between rounds patrolling the mall once it closed, Callahan wrote sentimental, inspirational one pagers. He was a late bloomer to writing. Back in grade school when the nuns ordered him to, "Write something!" he could only stare at a blank sheet of paper. He got so nervous that the thick, yellowish, wide-lined paper became a blur. Next thing he knew, he burped up a piece of the morning's breakfast on that smelly mildew paper. Turning in a miserable three sentences with a touch of vomit, he knew a good grade was not forthcoming.

Fast forward many years and Callahan loved to write when not engaged in his other favorite pastimes: eating, sleeping, reading, and working out. Callahan smiled to himself as he penned a congratulatory testimonial to a fellow mall cop who joined a police force, "I guess an old dog can learn new tricks," said Callahan to a wall of mementos and photos of people and places in a life well lived as he pecked on his keyboard.

Back at Willy's Water Hole when shifts ended, mall cops and the Callahan clan regrouped for free-roam conversations. Sharing ideas (no matter how absurd) and conversing with each other had become a lost art outside of Callahan & Company.

Callahan was usually the first to kick off the conversation. This evening his question to the group was, "If you had to pick the last day of your life, what would that be?"

Sammy immediately asked, "Why are we even talking about this?"

Callahan responded, "Of course you're not thinking about this. You're a young guy. Me on the other hand, I got to plan ahead."

Claire was a videographer by trade but she could have been a therapist. She probed for details asking, "So what day would that be?"

Callahan responded without hesitation, "New Year's Eve."

"Why, that's supposed to be a happy time?" responded Claire incredulously.

Callahan said, "Exactly my point. Why do you have to be happy at birthdays, merry at Christmas, and optimistic about the new year? Has anybody noticed we're on the cusp of another year of mayhem?"

"You got that right," chimed in Butch.

"There's something sad about singing 'Auld Lang Syne'," mused Callahan who seemed to be conversing more with himself than the gaggle of family and friends sprawled around the battered oak table in the back room.

Sammy sensed a flashback was on tap with a rant not far behind. Sure enough, Callahan continued, saying, " 'Auld Lang Syne' brings tears to my eyes, like when they play 'Amazing Grace' at funerals. I like to celebrate when I actually accomplish something. The best time in my life was when I got a scholarship for college. Better yet, there were days when I stuck it to some asshole bosses. Now those were good times that have nothing to do with New Year's Eve."

Bryce interjected, "I know what you mean. I don't need others telling me to be happy. I don't even like it when people tell me good luck. Are you telling us you're planning to kick the bucket and not ring in the new year?"

Callahan said, "I can't control that stuff. I'm just saying that December 31st is a clean break. No new tax year."

Sammy said, "Ugh, here we go again trying to save on money and taxes."

This got Kevin to thinking, "The best times are the unplanned, spontaneous events. Like remember the time we all got together a couple of days before Thanksgiving."

Sammy nodded, "Yea, good times except for the two Black Panthers who gave me shit 'cause I was in my Coast Guard uniform. Glad they haven't been back. At least it was good to regroup with former mall cops. Catching up with Wheeler was nice since he was back from his tour of duty in Africa."

"You know what's my favorite?" said Kevin. "Halloween at the Callahans when we used to rumble for hours beating each other up. Remember how we threw each other into piles of leaves, wearing extra clothing as padding. We were living in the moment with not a care in the world."

Callahan became unusually quiet when the last chuckle of remembrances drifted to the rafters like the smoke from the embers of the fireplace along the back wall.

"Now I'm using handrails when I go downstairs," lamented Callahan. "For years, I thought they were just decorations. Now, I pull on 'em sometimes, just to give me a little leverage going up stairs. Never used to do that."

Sammy asked the question everyone at the table was thinking, "So are you gonna be quitting the mall cop gig?"

"I'm hanging in there a bit longer. But you know what's really wearing me out?" responded Callahan.

"What's that?" asked Claire as she put on her coat but still wanted to know the source of Callahan's angst.

"I'm getting tired of everybody seeing no evil, hearing no evil, and speaking no evil. You're all staring into the eyes of the devil and it's time to speak up, listen up, and act up!"

Sammy said, "We got him on a roll now. Here we go again with good versus evil and the spiel about the devil lurking around."

"Damn right you are," said Callahan, "'cause I'm an Irish American. We're always keeping an eye on heaven while looking over our shoulder at the devil. Hey, that reminds me of an old Irish blessing."

"Why do Irish blessings and folktales always appear after the fifth beer?" asked Kevin.

"Shut up and let me finish my blessing," said Callahan. "Here it is: May you be in heaven a half hour before the devil knows you're dead. There, short and sweet. Now let's order another round of beer and get some sliders over here."

Chapter 23:
Callahan's Descent

The house was in total darkness. Sammy chuckled to himself, "Callahan's saving money again. He only lights up where he sits."

The bluish light of the TV flickered in the living room. Callahan sat sprawled back in his overstuffed chair, head back snoring up a storm. Bottles of Guinness sat on the coffee table next to the chair. A couple of empty bottles rolled under the table. Sammy frowned. Callahan's drinking formula was usually two and done. Seeing at least six bottles confirmed Claire's report he had accelerated alcohol intake since the passing of Maggie. She may have died but her credit card and medical bills stuck around to haunt Callahan. This was a pet peeve of Callahan's. He frequently ranted about how those who are frugal and healthy should not have to pay for those who went on spending and eating binges.

The TV channel was set at CNN with its steady stream of troublesome news. A shooting here and a shooting there followed by the hollow expression of condolences with no intention of getting to the root cause of madness. As Sammy tidied up so Callahan wouldn't trip over bottles upon waking from his slumber, he spotted an item more concerning than an empty bottle. It was Callahan's silver-plated snub nosed thirty-eight revolver. Normally it was locked away and used only when Callahan went for weekly target shooting. This evening it rested precariously on his lap. Sammy delicately lifted it since he noticed the safety was in the off position. As he returned the revolver to the safe, he spun the cylinder and was surprised to find only one bullet in the chamber. Callahan always kept the revolver fully stocked with six bullets. He called it his last line of defense, never missing an opportunity to describe how he would let the bastards get up close and unload at close range.

The hour was late. Sammy completed housekeeping chores, locked the front door, and crashed for the night in the spare bedroom. Tomorrow he would catch up with Callahan and maybe mention the one-bullet mystery. He also would contact Claire. She was filming a documentary in Greenland. Though she was stationed in a distant land, she usually had the inside scoop concerning Callahan.

Sammy set his alarm for 10:00 a.m. giving himself some much-needed sleep and some time to call Claire before Callahan woke up.

"What time is it up there?" asked Sammy in the most cherry voice he could muster.

"8:00 a.m. on a Saturday," replied Claire with groggy irritation.

"Sorry about the time change and early call but I wanted to give you a Callahan update," said Sammy who could no longer mask his anxiety.

"Is he setting landmines around the house?"

"Well, no, but he is the land mine. Last night I found him passed out in his chair with his snub nose perched on his lap."

"Not a good visual. Was it loaded?"

"Yea, but with only one bullet."

"He didn't discharge the other bullets in the house did he?"

"No, he's not that crazy. At least not yet. You talk to him more regularly than me. What's been bugging him, other than everything?"

"Well, I know he has days when he misses Maggie and I'm not just talking about her good cooking."

"Yea, we all miss that good cooking. And the house now has that old guy look. No flowers or plants. It's starting to look like a jail cell where all you do is eat, poop, and sleep."

"I wish we were around more to check in on him."

"I'm gonna see Butch and Ralph before I head back to finish my exams. Maybe they can make excuses to stop by from time to time."

"Too bad. It's not like the old days when everybody was around and nobody needed an invite to drop by."

"I heard the toilet flush. He must be up. I'll fill you in later. Say hi to the polar bears for me."

"OK, but they're few and far between. You be safe and good luck on exams. Love ya."

Callahan shuffled down the hallway in his ripped sweatpants and favorite sweatshirt sporting a Yale insignia which upon closer examination declared "Institute of the Sexually Gifted" with a subtitle that read "In Heatus Continuous." Sammy had a pot of coffee ready and toasted English muffins if he wanted them. Despite a headache and somewhat queasy stomach, Callahan ate his usual muffin topped with peanut butter and some apple slices.

Sammy tactfully asked, "How are you feeling?" to which Callahan snapped, "Do I look like I'm doing OK?"

Sammy knew now might not be the time and place to discuss the one-bullet revolver.

He let Callahan express his thoughts like a spool rolling out its thread.

Despite his headache, Callahan was in a surprisingly talkative mood.

"I was riding around during last night's shift listening to the Spanish speaking radio station. Thought I would teach myself Spanish. That lasted about a half an hour. I got bored and confused, catching only a word here and there."

"Maybe Santa will bring you one of those language learning modules, like the Rosetta Stone type stuff?" offered Sammy.

"Maybe Santa will bring me a lovely Latin lady who could teach me Spanish?"

Sammy groaned and thought to himself, leave that alone, don't encourage him.

"So I changed the station and landed on one of those financial planning channels," said Callahan as he munched on his muffin. "You know, the talk shows about flipping houses, investing wisely, and retiring happily into the sunset. What a pile of crap! The advice was good but the callers got under my skin. Complaining about how they weren't happy and weren't making enough money. I shoulda called in and told them my situation. They all seemed worried about keeping up with the Joneses. Who the hell are these Joneses? I say the hell with them. That's when I switched channels again."

"So where did that lead you?" asked Sammy, fearing where this was going.

"I landed on one of those angry talk radio stations. They were spouting venom on both sides of the political spectrum. I can only stomach these shows for short intervals. But I listen to 'em. You know why?"

"Tell me, why do you punish yourself?"

"Because it's like watching a football team so you know how to beat them. The final straw was when a listener posed the following question: What's worse than a nigger or a Jew?

"I thought to myself, this should be interesting. Both groups are in the cross hairs of bigotry, so what could be worse?

"The caller answered his own question stating, 'It's a cop.'

"That's when I knew I was listening to a patriot prider."

"I've met a few of them in my travels," lamented Sammy. "They bounce from anarchy to conspiracy. Their message is trust no one and stop the world, I want to get off."

Callahan concluded, "That was my cue to give up on the radio for the balance of the shift."

Since Sammy had been finishing up his studies in Oxford, England and had not visited Callahan for a while, he opted to listen and let Callahan continue his ranting.

Callahan lamented that time had taken its toll. Days blurred into weeks and months ultimately into years. He couldn't fathom the fact he had worked over fifteen years as a weekend mall cop. For him, work had become an end in and of itself. The job had become a means of paying bills with no particular goal beyond this. He began referring to himself as the new American serf, the new American indentured servant.

"I'm thinking maybe I'd be better off in jail. At least they give you three hots and a cot. Then again, the threat of being violated is a downside."

"Did you ever think, in a way, we're all in jail?" pondered Sammy, trying to move Callahan to higher philosophical ground.

"I'm outside of jail but I'm still a prisoner of my bills. Ain't that crazy? In jail I get sick and they patch me up. Outside of jail, I pay crazy high health insurance and co-payments. Go figure, where's the freedom on the outside? Maybe I should just don a hospital smock and turn myself into the state capitol, declaring myself a ward of the state."

"Let me know how that turns out," said Sammy as he encouraged him to have another muffin and cup of coffee. There was no consoling a man with a hangover on such a rant.

Chapter 24:
You Are Not Alone

Sammy had to get back to Oxford University for the home stretch of the semester. Before leaving, he placed a call to Uncle Butch to line up chaperones for Callahan.

"Hi, Butch, it's Sammy."

"Hey, Sammy, great to hear from you. Have you met any nice girls in England? Maybe you could marry royalty."

"No such luck, but that's OK, some of those royals can be high maintenance. How's everything in the States?" asked Sammy in the cheeriest British accent he could muster.

"Moving every day closer to a federation over here instead of a nation," said Butch glumly.

"You think the USA will become like the EU. Same currency but otherwise separate but equal?" asked Sammy.

"You're the international scholar, what do you think? I'm not sure how equal these states are gonna be when this ship breaks up. Whole sections are gonna be barefoot, pregnant, gun toting, and foul mouthed."

"Sounds like you're describing the mall," laughed Sammy.

"It has its good days and bad days. Depends on what's scheduled. One day an art show and another day a shooting. This thing between the Aliens and the Anarchists is really getting out of control. Have you heard about it over there?"

"Yea, it's been in the news and we're having the same thing here. Jolly old England's not so jolly."

"Enough international stuff. How are you doing?" asked Butch.

"I'm OK, I'm getting a tutor to help with statistics. Numbers were never my thing but the rest of the subjects are all A's."

"Good for you. Keep up the good work. How's the social life?"

"It's fine on campus. You wouldn't believe the mix of backgrounds here. For the first time in my life, I don't have to start every conversation explaining my roots."

"What about off-campus?"

"That's a different story. You have to watch your back when you're at the local pub. Get that look from the locals. The town versus gown thing," said Sammy.

"Don't be roaming around alone over there. Remember strength in numbers. It's gotten the same way over here. Can't trust anybody. Everybody in the USA has a flag sticker on their car. I love my country but I don't need to be reminded of where I live every time I open the driver's door."

"Over here they got the Union Jack on everything, especially since they broke away from the EU and the Scots are always threatening to break away."

"Same old, same old here in the US, I keep working my ass off and telling people when they're full of shit. I wish there was a flag for that."

"How about that coat of arms Callahan was having his artist friend concoct. You know, the one with the eagle's talons digging into the head of the banker man and the mugger?"

"He's still working on it. They're trying to come up with a logo. Kicking around the phrase 'tough love'."

"Anyways," said Sammy drawing in a deep breath, "I wanted to ask you and Ralph and whoever else is around to keep tabs on Callahan. He's showing more signs of going off the rails."

"Sure thing. We're super busy with the eat-sleep-work routine, especially since it costs an arm and leg to buy anything. I'm not sure how much longer the mall can last."

"I know what you mean," replied Sammy. He was tempted to mention Callahan's condition the other night but like most conversations, some topics get swept under the rug.

"I'll be sure to tell Ralph," assured Butch. "I almost forgot to mention that Captain Wheeler is back in the area. He retired from the army and set up a shop in BellHaven. Lucky bastard. I wish I put in twenty years, got a decent pension, and started a new life. No wife and no kids. Travel the world and be flush with cash."

"Good for Wheeler. Be sure to give him my regards. Don't be too hard on yourself. You went all these years without getting arrested and you kept me on track."

"Keep it that way and don't do anything I wouldn't," said Butch in the gruffest voice he could muster, masking his deep concern for Sammy as he signed off.

It didn't take long for Captain Wheeler to make his surprise visit to Callahan.

"Who the hell is banging on my door this late?" muttered Callahan, rousing from a dream of the mall covered in poison ivy. Some nights he enjoyed drifting off to sleep just as twilight set in and darkness filled the house. Peeking through the curtain covering the cracked window of the front door, he saw the silhouette of a man wearing an army fatigue jacket displaying an African Corp insignia.

Flinging open the door, he exclaimed, "Well I'll be damned, look what the cat dropped on my doorstep!"

"Sorry to have woken you and banging on the door," apologized Captain Wheeler who quickly added, "it's only 8:00 p.m., I thought you'd still be up."

"Don't worry about it. There's no need to fix a doorbell when guests are few and far between. I'm still working the weekend mall cop shift. I got to tell you, when I get home from the office job after fighting the traffic, I go straight to bed. No dinner. No nothing."

"I know what you mean," said Wheeler with reflexive sympathy.

"Don't trip over the boxes," warned Callahan, weaving his way through the dimly lit maize. "I'm still sorting out Maggie's shit, deciding what to keep. Also keeping the lights off. Why give United Illuminating any more money than they need?"

Wheeler dutifully followed, having flashbacks to picking through the African jungle, entering a clearing, which in this case was Callahan's kitchen.

Callahan flicked on the kitchen light and fished for plates and cups. "It's nice to have some company. Gives me a reason to make a pot of coffee."

While Callahan tended to that task, Wheeler scanned the kitchen, recalling rowdy conversations among odd-ball mixtures of guests. He smiled to himself when it dawned on him that the mall was the link that brought them together. The collective adoption of Sammy was the glue. Wheeler's pleasant reflection was interrupted when Callahan plopped an Entiments Danish roll in the middle of the table with encouragement to, "Help yourself."

Wheeler recalled how Maggie used to have place settings, homemade baked pies, and a fresh cut floral bouquet at the ready to greet guests. As Callahan sniffed the milk carton to make sure it had not soured, Wheeler noticed how sparse Callahan's living space had become. Wheeler was in the presence of a man who had packed his bags for a trip.

"Do you want me to reset the time on the microwave clock?" offered Wheeler.

"That's OK, I got used to it being an hour off. I've gotten used to a lot of stuff being off," said Callahan with his back to Wheeler as he spilled some coffee grounds while spooning them into the filter.

"So what's your plan?" asked Wheeler, instinctively migrating to a wooden chair that was still missing an arm after all these years. "Are you gonna be the oldest mall cop in America? Seems like you're working yourself into an early grave, like the rest of us."

Ignoring Wheeler's reference to Father Time, Callahan asked, "When did you get back from Africa and why aren't you in uniform?"

"I'm done, retired from the army. I started a consulting firm right here in BellHaven. I tried to fix up the third world. Now I'm trying to fix up this third-world city."

"Good luck with that. Exactly what type of consulting, or is this some secret black ops thing?"

"If I tell ya, I gotta kill ya," kidded Wheeler.

"Anyways, it's great to see you again," said Callahan, lopping off a corner of the danish. "This has been a strange week. One day Butch stopped by and another day Ralph drops in on the excuse he happened to be 'in the neighborhood'. I see these guys when I work my weekend shift. Got me wondering if there's a sign at the end of the street announcing 'Free Stuff at Callahan's'."

"Did they ask you for money?"

"No, why?

"Then maybe they just wanted to make sure you're OK. Maybe they wanted to let you know that they care about you."

"Why do you say that?" asked Callahan. "Do I look like somebody that needs to be looked after? Somebody who cannot take care of himself?"

"Of course not. Hey, let me tell you why I'm back and what I'm up to?"

"Yea, what brings you to these parts? I thought they would bury you in the army uniform."

"I put in my time and got a decent pension. I did as much as I could in Africa. Now I want to apply community building skills in BellHaven."

"So what's your plan?" asked Callahan, leaning forward in his chair, dabbing a wet paper towel removing spaghetti sauce remnants on one of the year-round Christmas placemats.

"In Africa you have warlords. In BellHaven you have gangs," explained Wheeler.

"Tell me about it, we see the wannabes in the mall."

"In Africa we secure the villages, establish a perimeter, make sure everybody is safe, fed, educated, and busy."

"So what's that got to do with BellHaven?"

"We have to do the same thing on a neighborhood level here in the USA. Why are rich people the only ones who have gated communities, personal tutors, personal trainers, personal chefs, and privileges?"

"So are you gonna convert ghettos into lifestyles of the rich and famous?"

"No, but once you give people a sense that they control their space and they control their lives, they become self-sufficient and thrive. Grow their own gardens, run their own businesses. You know what I mean?"

"What happened to the glass-half-empty guy I knew way back when we discovered Sammy? Remember how you used to push rowdy kids out to the bus shelter claiming they would eat each other up? Thin out the herd. Now you're saying you're trying to heal the herd?"

"I guess I saw how bad it is overseas. I tried things out over there and it might work right here. You know what else I realized?"

"What's that?

"All these years keeping track of Callahan & Company made me think that working together on a common cause is the only way we'll survive."

"I guess you're right," said Callahan, stroking a beard in dire need of trimming. "I'm even thinking about becoming a school mentor once my measly Social Security kicks in. Once I quit being a mall cop. I was certified to teach social studies when I graduated from college a hundred years ago. Never got hired."

"Just think of all those young minds you could have corrupted," teased Wheeler.

Ignoring Wheeler's jab, Callahan plunged on saying, "Maybe I could help you out with your community building scheme."

"I'd love to add you to my team."

"Just keep in mind that I'm tired and you guys have to carry on."

"Speaking of building a team, I wanted to reach out to the mall alumni. Fill me in on who's doing what."

"Well, Nicco's on a couple of wait lists for police departments. He got a good shot at joining BellHaven and Northville.

"There's pros and cons to each," said Wheeler. "BellHaven will give him plenty of action but they pay less. Makes no sense. High crime urban cops get paid less than suburban cops sitting in parking lots. Northville might be more relaxing in the long term, like when he gets old like you."

"Very funny, wise guy," shot back Callahan. "No matter what department he joins, I hate the thought of him getting stuck in golden cufflinks. He might put in years and be unhappy. Worse yet, he might end up being the only clean cop."

"I remember when Nicco was a rookie, he was a bit of a hothead. Seemed to have in for the black kids," said Wheeler.

"He's mellowed. I'll give you an example. We were babysitting a foul-mouthed punk held in the police sub-station after a fight. Kid couldn't be more than twelve years old. Cussing everybody out. Called one cop ugly and called me old."

"Well he got that part right, go on," teased Wheeler.

"Well, one of the cops asks him if there's any parent or guardian who can pick him up. He says no. The cop asks him again and emphasizes the word 'anybody'.

"He shouts, 'Nobody,' and scowls at the cop who leans forward into his personal space asking if maybe a dad could pick him up. I'm not sure if the cop was genuinely interested in counseling this kid or if he was just trying to get a rise out of him."

"Sounds like the latter. Like poking the tiger with a stick through the bars," said Wheeler as he shifted in his wooden, cushion-less seat.

Callahan was oblivious to Wheeler's discomfort and plunged ahead saying, "Nicco turned to me after we left the substation, saying, 'That kid just needs a good cry.' Who knew Nicco grew a heart and loosened his fist?"

"How long do you think he would last as a cop?" asked Wheeler with renewed interest.

"That depends on him. It depends on whether anybody wants to be a cop anymore. Everybody hates you. Everybody's playing Monday Morning Quarterback."

"Maybe Nicco can put a few cop years under his belt. Then get involved in the security part of my community building," offered Wheeler.

"That's what I have been telling all you guys these years," exclaimed Callahan. You got to have a Plan B. Have options in place for when they ultimately screw you. Think about every time you quit a job working for a son-of-a-bitch and had something else lined up."

"Ahh, that's the Callahan curmudgeon I knew. Nice to know that some things never change. Speaking of changes, whatever happened to Junior and all his conspiracy theories? Don't tell me he's now a CEO somewhere."

"Last I heard, he went west to become a survivalist. I saw that coming. I just hope he didn't join one of the whackadoo cults that sprung up when the economy went south."

"Maybe you'll be pleasantly surprised and receive one of those Christmas postcards displaying the perfect wife, kids, and pets in exotic locations," said Wheeler as he sipped his coffee.

"And maybe pigs will fly. You want another coffee?" asked Callahan when it appeared he and Wheeler were talked out.

"One more and then I got to run," said Wheeler as he glanced at his watch.

"I have one last weird question," asked Callahan in a tenuous tone.

"Shoot," said Wheeler.

"Did you see lots of lions in Africa?"

"Sure, why?"

"I've been having weird dreams about them. Some of them lurk on the edge of the jungle ready to pounce on the weak and sick. Some just kill for fun. They don't bother to eat the carcass. They just kill other lions."

"Yea, you're definitely ready to hang up your service belt and quit the mall cop scene," said Wheeler, leaning back in his chair, taking full measure of Callahan.

"It's like we're living in the jungle and lions are circling around," said Callanhan as he stirred his coffee, oblivious to Wheeler's stare."

"You know what the solution is?" offered Wheeler, sizing up Callahan. "I've seen this happen in Africa. We should do it in the good old USA."

"Tell me, oh great and wise world traveler," said Callahan, extending his hands in a deferential bow.

"We need to band together. There's strength in numbers. Solidarity and teamwork can overcome anything. Remember how we used to share stories from the Animal Channel and History Channel?"

"Yea, what's that got to do with my lion dreams."

"Fish form schools, zebras form herds, wolves hunt in packs. They protect each other. They work together. Humans do the opposite. Did you notice how on the History Channel, they fight each other? Why? Because we're too pig-headed, proud, and independent to put aside our differences."

"Wheeler, that's what I always liked about you. Always looking at the big picture and connecting the dots. Who knew mall cops could be so smart."

"On that note of confidence, I got to go. Thanks for the danish and coffee," said Wheeler as he started to give Callahan a hug that morphed into a handshake.

"Enjoyed seeing you and catching up," responded Callahan with an awkward pat on the back of Wheeler's leather jacket as he lumbered down the dark paneled hallway devoid of any artwork. "Thanks to you, the lions will not visit me tonight."

Chapter 25:
The Devil on Christmas Eve

Mall management and local politicians wanted this Christmas Eve to be special. Elementary school students from BellHaven clad in tan pants and maroon shirts shuffled into the food court like hostages rounded up for a press conference. Nicco commented under his breath to Callahan, "They looked more like defendants appearing at court than darlings preparing to sing 'Joy to the World'."

Callahan said in a hushed tone, "Check out how chaperones lining up alternating rows of BellHaven kids and suburban kids."

"Ebony and ivory in perfect harmony," quipped Nicco.

Chaperones circled like sheep dogs corralling stragglers at the end of rows and verbally nipping at the class clowns to keep their hands and feet to themselves.

As soon as music teachers exited from a huddle, they announced that the choir was as ready as it ever would be. With a nod to Bob Sutherland, the mall director, ceremonies commenced.

Bob tapped the microphone, adjusting it to his six-foot, three-inch frame. "Ladies and Gentlemen!" he bellowed in the best ringmaster voice he could muster.

"He must think he's P.T. Barnum," said Callahan in a sidewise nod to Nicco.

"Greatest show on Earth right here in Renaissance Mall," whispered back Nicco.

"Let's just see if these kids can make Christmas special again," said Callahan.

The trumpeter sounded that first beat of "Joy to the World" and children belted out the stanzas.

"Not exactly the Mormon Tabernacle Choir but not bad," said the mall manager to Callahan as he slipped away from the crowd enroute to meet the manager of Macy's. "Seems like they hired their Santa from Alcoholics-R-Us," said Bob as he rushed off to clean up another Santa mess.

Callahan reminded himself to scan the audience, thinking, I'm a mall cop. I'm supposed to be watching for trouble. But what am I looking for? There's nuts and haters everywhere. It's not like they're wearing nuts and haters uniforms. Could it be the bald white guy staring off into the distance like he's not even at this event? Probably not. He actually looks like me. Maybe it's the soccer mom who looks exhausted hovering over her toddler twins. She's somebody who could snap, thought Callahan as he recalled hectic times raising his own twins.

Callahan's daydreaming was interrupted when a helicopter mom adamantly asked if the mall was closing at 6:00 p.m. Callahan assured her that there would be plenty of time to tuck the darlings into bed well before

St. Nick's midnight visit. What annoyed him was her indignation that her Northville cherubs were lined up cheek to jaw with these BellHaven ruffians. Why does everybody have an attitude about everybody else? thought Callahan.

I can't change all that, just focus on the singing, thought Callahan as he redirected his gaze to the innocent faces of second and third graders with their angelic voices singing traditional melodies of "Silent Night" and "Oh Holy Night." A tear welled up in his eye as he noticed the crowd settle into the melody.

He had a second reason to tear up. He missed his late wife and kids, including Sammy who he considered his own even though he was officially only his guardian. All the kids were off doing their own thing. Claire, Kevin, Bryce, and Bruce were just starting their careers and were scattered far and wide. Sammy was a Rhodes Scholar attending Oxford University in England.

Kevin had just started working for a progressive think tank in D.C. defending the First Amendment, which had been under attack for the last ten years by revisionists who claimed to be the true American patriots. Despite a full schedule attending law school at night, Kevin called Callahan regularly to discuss what they described as "State of the Unions".

Kevin's twin sister, Claire, was in Greenland helping a crew with a documentary concerning the impact of global warming. Greenland's population had tripled in recent years because vast frozen areas heretofore uninhabitable were gradually becoming prime real estate for humans. As with Kevin's State of the Union chats, conversations with Claire included world affairs and a healthy dose of ripping on the "powers that be" who insisted that global warming was but a figment of misguided imaginations. Claire described seeing polar bear carcasses floating in water that used to be icebergs.

Bruce had just started working on a virtual reality game in NYC with Gotham as the backdrop. Callahan had a flashback to the time when Bruce's third-grade teacher asked students what they wanted to be when they grew up. There was the usual listing of cops, firemen, and nurses. When it was Bruce's turn, Callahan chuckled to himself recalling that Bruce announced he wanted to be a dictator. Bruce's desk was moved next to the teacher's desk as a precautionary move for the rest of that school year. It only made sense that Bruce managed to blend his love of history with his thirst for power, creating gaming experiences that were action packed and educational. He and Callahan used to joke about his projects as being "violence with a purpose". Callahan recalled suggesting ultra-violent scenes to which Bruce politely said he would "take into consideration".

Bryce, the physicist, was stationed in France, fulfilling a childhood dream of working on an atomic simulator. Bryce was always smashing up things at home so now he got to pick on the world's smallest particles. Like father, like son, Callahan thought, since his own nickname as a kid was Destructo.

Lastly, Sammy was finishing up his year at Oxford University. His career in the US Coast Guard enabled him to travel around the world. Technical skills learned on ships coupled with interpersonal skills honed at exotic ports prepared him for life's challenges at home, abroad, and in his personal life. Oxford University developed his skills as a thinker, speaker, and philosopher. Callahan marveled at how Sammy evolved into a young renaissance man. This was a term of endearment that the extended clan assigned to Sammy, but never to his face since taking oneself too seriously was a cardinal sin in the Callahan household.

Snowflakes gently fell on car windshields. Soft, fluffy, big flakes of snow. The kind of snow kids like to catch on their tongues. The perfect atmosphere for carolers singing their hearts out and sales clerks ringing up last-minute sales.

Not so for Steffan, who grudgingly turned on the wipers of his beat-up red Buick. For him the snow was nothing more than an annoyance. He needed a better view of his point of entry. He was oblivious to the weather. Oblivious to everything. Only the mission mattered. He despised it all.

The snow.

The singing.

Everything.

He blasted "Psycho Zoo" one last time before gathering up his tools of the trade.

This was the moment he simulated for months in the darkened isolation of his parents' basement. Finally he would be somebody. He would end the hypocrisy. He will be remembered forever. There was no cataclysmic event that triggered his downward spiral which began over ten years ago. He was not a tortured refugee from some god-awful war-torn land. He was not like the Lost

Boys of Somalia who managed to get to America ten years ago and strived to "Make America Great".

Was he bullied as a youngster? Rumor was that he was pushed around but to what extent is not known.

Was it shyness? Depression? Social awkwardness?

Was it his parents' divorce?

Was it a rebuff by a girl in his first year in high school?

We will never know.

It was later found out that when his dad's dog Americus died, that was the final straw for Steffan. Ironically, this animal was his only connection to humanity. All humans in his life let him down. Too bad his old man didn't die instead of the dog. He was a useless, hateful piece of shit that smacked around Steffan at every opportunity. The Buick was almost out of gas and so was Steffan. He had no exit strategy. No Plan B.

He dined on a steady diet of ultra-violent video games. Reality blurred with fantasy.

When did the drum beat of racist, misogynistic websites twist his mind and world view? This we will never know.

On this holy night, Steffan believed in his dark heart that he would give birth, as described in his manifesto, to a new world order, one of his own creations. He would be the dictator. After tonight, Steffan would rid the world of all things superficially spiritual.

He would silence that awful singing.

And so he did.

Unleashing the fury of his AR-15, mowing down twenty-five children as they struck the last chorus of "Oh Holy Night".

Rookie Nicco didn't have a chance, immediately taking a bullet to the head.

Callahan scrambled to get a shot off but his right arm (shooting arm) took a bullet from the spray. Stumbling backward and slumping against the wall, he realized his right thigh had been severed. He lost consciousness in a pool of blood. His own and the children's.

Ralph had the good fortune (if you can call it that) to be out of the line of fire behind a pillar. He was on his coffee break. Being a veteran of many fist fights, knife fights, and years of military service handling firearms, he was in the right place, right time. He dropped the coffee and dropped the assassin with several shots to his head and upper body. The shot directly to the forehead terminated the evil but the senseless carnage was completed. The other four shots from Ralph's Glock landing on the body armor of Stefan's torso were pure adrenaline: Ralph was plugging a corpse. Callahan and at least fifteen severely injured persons were whisked to St. Andrew's Hospital and other area hospitals. An on-site morgue was set up for the rest.

Callahan's kids had planned a Christmas Day surprise. They were staying nearby at Uncle Gabriel (a.k.a. Superman's) house. Since it was Superman's insistence that Sammy be raised under the guardianship of Callahan with the crew of uncles and aunts playing supporting roles, he felt obligated to work behind the scenes to make sure that the guardianship survived. Since he was one of the original authors of the contract of mutual aid crafted after Sammy was discovered in the bathroom, he planned events a couple of times during the year, making sure the glue of the contract remained strong.

The plan was for Callahan's kids and Sammy to ring Callahan's doorbell bearing presents and bring him to lunch at noon on Christmas Day. Instead, they held a vigil at his bedside at St. Andrew's Hospital. He was gravely ill and drifted in and out of consciousness. During one of his more lucid moments, he whispered to the bedside vigil, "How was Nicco doing?" In the fog of war when all hell broke loose in the food court, he recalled Nicco getting hit before him. When told of Nicco's death, his silence was deafening. He gazed to a distant place that only he would know. Quietly, almost inaudibly, he expressed remorse that he was alive and rookie Nicco was dead. He said with bitterness that the kid had his whole life ahead of him. Why couldn't he be dead and take his place?

Callahan's remorse went beyond the usual survivor's guilt. He revealed a secret that he kept to himself for at least six months. He only had six months to live. The diagnosis of cancer of the esophagus had spread to the lungs. Since he already had one foot in the grave, his death could have been a replacement for Nicco's and the children. Why couldn't his death be an offering or a bargaining chip with the Almighty God? Why couldn't there be some sort of negotiation with the Almighty? Why did this young officer and all those innocent children have to die when he could have taken their place? What kind of god allows this? Is there even a god?

This was Callahan's last rant. His breath became even more shallow but he had just enough energy to tell his daughter and four sons that he loved them and was very proud of them. Sammy happened to be sitting closest and heard him whisper that he was very tired.

Sammy whispered back, "You did your best, you earned a long, well deserved rest." With that, Callahan peacefully closed his eyes and drifted off.

Chapter 26:
The Gathering, the Eulogy, the Promise

The line of mourners extended out the double doors of Coughlin's Funeral Home. Red-white-blue arm bands were distributed upon entry. Callahan and Nicco's families insisted on them as a demonstration of patriotic solidarity confronting dark forces. Butch and Ralph were hunkered down in the sitting room set off to the right of the viewing room. In years past, this was the smoking room. Now it's the ruminating room. They furtively directed darts toward persons they considered phonies. "I'd like to wrap that guy in the mouth," said Butch as he spotted an old Polack who screwed him on a business venture years ago.

"Leave it alone," cautioned Ralph. "We got bigger fish to fry. Save our energy for guttin' the real enemy," admonished Ralph seething with post-massacre anger.

In the sitting room to the left of the viewing room, coffee and pastries were piled high on white-linen covered tables decorated with green carnations in shamrock formations. Not on display, but ever present, were stronger drinks sipped from flasks discreetly carried in jacket pockets of husky, red-faced male mourners. Stories of Callahan's antics were bantered about while jokes were exchanged in as discreet and respectful a manner as possible in the hushed confines of a funeral parlor.

"How are you holding up?" Kevin asked Claire during a rare break in the "Sorry for your troubles" receiving line routine.

"Putting on a good show, it's what us Irish do best," said Claire with puffy eyes staring ahead to nothing in particular.

Once the public calling hours concluded, the seating area was reserved for family members for final viewing and remembrances. The traditional Irish wake with its focus on remembrances was replaced by a new Irish wake focused on revenge and survival.

Claire broke the silence announcing, "I'm not speaking tomorrow. I'm in no condition. I'm too angry."

"Count us out too," said Kevin and Bryce. Kevin added, "Is it a sin to denounce God in his own house? What's the penalty for cursing in church?"

"We're Irish, we compartmentalize. That's what we'll do tomorrow," said Bruce. "What's that Irish saying? Don't get mad, get even. Well it's time to do both. Are the rest of you on board?"

"Count me in. I'm just waiting to get past tomorrow," said Bryce. "I used to think twice, give people a break, give 'em a second chance. No more playing nice for me."

Sammy continued to stare at the casket as he slouched in a wooden chair positioned facing the casket. His siblings were gathered in a circle of overstuffed chairs facing away from the casket.

"I say Sammy does the eulogy tomorrow. We're all too worked up. Sammy, are you OK with this?"

No response from Sammy.

"We'll be there to support you but we can't bring ourselves to speak nicely," said Bruce.

Sammy snapped out of his trance. That wasn't the only thing that snapped. "So I'm nothing more than a show dog tomorrow. Trotted out to perform tricks. All my life it's been Sammy the exceptional. Sammy the different one. Sammy the one who came from nothing to become something. When can Sammy just be Sammy? I'm hurting like the rest of you."

"I didn't mean it that way," said Bruce. "It's just that you have the discipline to hold it together. You have the voice to pull us through this. If each of us speaks, we'll be there all day. Worse yet, things will be said that can't be taken back."

"So when do I get to grieve, to let it all out?" said Sammy.

"Once we get through tomorrow, we're all gonna regroup. We'll reminisce, just like Callahan would want us to do, down at Willy's Water Hole and over at Burpee's Diner," offered Bryce.

"And mark my words, we'll never forget. We'll avenge his death," added Claire. "When mad dogs foam at the mouth, we take off the safety, unload the clip, shoot to kill."

"Remember Callahan's crazy ideas about arming everyone with a grenade? Maybe he wasn't so crazy," said Kevin with a nervous giggle.

"Don't get me wrong," said Claire. "I'll still believe five-year-olds can be normal humans. But I swear to God, once they turn mutant, I'll terminate them."

"You got that right, sis" said Bruce who by now was pacing along the back wall of the room like a caged wolf. "From now on we move together in formation as a pack. Nobody is caught alone. It'll be like our ancestors who didn't venture out of the village and beyond the treeline at night."

"We all carry panic buttons, like the commercial with the old lady yelling, 'I've fallen and I can't get up!', except the button summons the rest of us," said Bryce in pep rally mode. "We'll be the New England Minutemen answering the call with AR-15s instead of muskets. Blast them before they get a shot off."

"OK, OK, I'll do the eulogy tomorrow," said Sammy, "but enough with all this crazy talk. Just so I know, who are all these people we're gonna blast?"

"It's anybody. That's what's scary. They come in all colors and sizes. They went to school with us. Most of them speak the same language. None of them can be trusted. We need to smell 'em out when they mutate," said Claire.

"We're at war," added Kevin. "From now on there's no more gathering with strangers, no more children singing carols. We got to keep strangers at arm's length till they can be trusted."

"That's a hell of a way to live out our lives," said Sammy.

"It's how you survive in wartime," said Kevin. "Callahan always told us to cross-train, have a Plan B, and think like survivalists. We need to take it to the next level.

We're gonna go back to our jobs but from now on we have to watch our backs. We'll have weapons at the ready to snuff out haters whomever they may be. No more Mr. Nice Guy for Callahan & Company."

"Sounds like a plan," said Sammy who realized he had to come up with a eulogy that would be both inspirational and a call to action. Staring at the ceiling before drifting off to sleep that night, he titled his eulogy "War and Peace".

On the morning of the funeral, the air was crisp, the sky was clear. There was an unusual quietness amid a gathering of so many people in the cavernous space of the cathedral. Gone was the chatty undertow of conversations. The stoic silence was a mixture of sheer rage at the senselessness of the massacre and a resolution to do something, anything to stop this madness.

Sammy strode slowly and confidently to the pulpit in his Coast Guard dress blues. A navy blue dress jacket decked out with a single row of polished gold buttons. Military drills in Groton and oratory practice at Oxford prepared him for this day.

As Sammy scanned the congregation, he spotted Captain Wheeler in the front row also decked out in his army dress blue uniform. Both Sammy and Wheeler's service days were over but hauling out their uniforms just seemed like the right thing to do. A war had been launched. Uniforms symbolized that line in the sand that begged to be drawn. Being a Rhodes Scholar at Oxford required no uniform but Sammy thought to himself, there's a uniform worn by everyone's school, everyone's workplace, everyone's family. It's a uniform that grounds them for whatever curve ball life throws at them. To-day's a hell of a curve ball, he thought, inhaling deeply to steady his nerves.

St. Katherine's cathedral was packed for the dual funeral of veteran Callahan and rookie Nicco. Their families agreed that tandem funerals were appropriate since they worked together and died together. They came from different worlds. One was old, the other was young. One was highly educated with a master's degree and the other was midway to obtaining his criminal justice degree. Their cultures were different but they shared a work ethic and a sense of what was right and what was wrong.

The sea of mourners included the traditional dark suits and black ties. White shirts on men and black dresses on women. For Sammy they resembled rows of black birds perched solemnly on high wires. Their conservative, traditional drabness, contrasted with the bright, floral moomoos of women in the first four rows near the altar. They were the friends of Nicco's mother, showing their support reflecting Hawaiian roots on his maternal side. Sammy was struck by the thought that garb and styles vary but the sorrow is all the same. Race and ancestry may differ but tears are all the same color.

For a fleeting moment, Sammy fixated on the two caskets that resembled a mini train. One was covered by a US flag topped off with green carnations in the shape of a shamrock and the other draped with the Puerto Rican flag with maroon leis sprinkled over it.

As Sammy gazed over the standing-room-only congregation numbering over one thousand, he was in awe of the diversity and solidarity of the assembly. There were people from every walk of life. There were rich, poor, and everything in between. Somber, traditional funeral attire dominated the central pews but along the fringes and packed in the vestibules were additional mourners. Here were the members of the mall's cleaning crew in their gray tunics with dark blue trim. Here were the employees of the mall's stores in outfits ranging from tailored chic to pop street. There were liberals, conservatives, left wing, right wing, and no wing at all. The one thing the entire congregation had in common was sadness and anger. As Sammy drew a deep breath to launch his eulogy, he realized that this eclectic collage of humanity was what Callahan fondly referred to as "The Base". The real people. The people that do the work, showing up every day and somehow move from sunrise to sunset to see another day and make another dollar.

"Let us not let the evil of one snuff out the positive of the many," announced Sammy with confidence and clarity. "Callahan and Nicco would have wanted it that way. Why do we only come together in times of sadness? Callahan used to say, 'I enjoy a good Irish wake but I'd much rather visit the dead while they're alive'."

A nervous chuckle rolled through the congregation. The ripple that follows fond reflections of the departed.

Switching gears and tearing into the meat of his message, Sammy posed the following questions, "When the procession is over and the caskets are lowered, where will you go? What will you do? Back to your couches for binge watching or the bar for binge drinking. Will you gamers wear out your thumbs on the controllers? How important will your text messages and email be after today?"

Foreheads throughout the congregation tilted slightly forward. Eyes cast downward. Minds raced to avoid the harsh truth that more could be done. Things had to change. But how?

Sammy's remembrances cascaded forth. "Callahan was a history buff. He would haunt me if I didn't make reference to the Irish Rebellion of 1912. Also known as the Easter Rebellion. For those needing a history refresher," he continued, "the leaders of the Irish Rebellion in 1912 established an independent Irish nation. They were slowly and systematically executed by British overlords. Although the British resoundingly crushed the rebellion, the execution of these rebels elevated them to martyr status. This galvanized the Irish independence movement, paving the way to ultimate success."

"So when does our rebellion start? When will these martyrs, the old mall cop, the young mall cop, and the innocent children get the justice they deserve? The justice that only we can assure them. Can you promise me on this cold New England day that from this day forward we shall not look away?

"We shall not look away from the damaged soul that spiraled into hell. The human wreck that sacrificed these innocents. When did he lose his humanity? Where is our resolve to prevent the hate virus from bringing another soul down that dark path to perdition?

"After today, will we continue to look away from the ugly face of racism and intolerance? Will we make believe it's not there? Or, shall we stop it in its tracks? Cut off the head of that snake before it gets a foothold in our thoughts, words or actions.

"After today, will we continue to avert each other's eyes when we know we're damaged and hurting? From this day forward, will we pledge to have each other's backs, knowing that if we don't we'll be picked off, one by one, by the evil one who lies, divides and conquers."

Spontaneous amens and intermittent clapping greeted Sammy's call to action and his exhortation to never forget the massacre at Renaissance Center.

"Reach out, heal the Lost Ones for whom there remains some chance of redemption. And remember," he continued, "we've all been down this road before. Everybody here has roots that run deep. Roots that have survived poisoned soil. As someone who is half black, I take inspiration from the trials and tribulations of my enslaved ancestors who survived the horrific Middle Passage. More recently in world history, there was the assassination of Dr. Martin Luther King Jr. Let the martyrdom of Dr. King and countless others from every race and religion who have defiantly stared into the face of hate and injustice be an inspiration to do what's needed when it's most needed. This is the promise that I proposed today.

"Are you ready to leave here to confront that dark and foreboding world?"

On this note, hands clapped and eyes watered.

As the procession slowly exited the church with bagpipes dutifully blaring "Amazing Grace", snow pelted the caskets. This was a typical New England snow squall. Temporary in time but with an intensity that's an ominous reminder of blizzards to come. Uncle Butch who was more known for fighting than speaking quipped,

"This was a Callahan type of day. A Gotham type of day. Cold, gray, and edgy. Callahan always described himself as a winter dog, a husky who enjoyed the first blast of cold signaling the onset of winter." Gazing upward, Uncle Butch observed, "The skies to the south are solidly gray and foreboding but to the north there's a patch of royal blue breaking through that grip of gray."

Only time and events would tell if the royal blue would overcome the numbing gray. Only time and events will tell if the promise will be kept.

The End

If you enjoyed the book, please leave a review
at your online store or Goodreads.

Keep in touch with Greg at:
www.dunnwriteswell.com

Acknowledgments

To my parents who provided a safe, encouraging, loving launch pad for life's journey.

To family members, past and present, whose conversations triggered ideas and brought levity to my darkest moments.

To all persons I have worked with and encountered since that day when I realized I'm not the center of the universe.

Collectively, all of the above compose the mosaic of experiences, thoughts and emotions that are baked into this novel and for that I am ever so grateful.

About the Author

Greg spent the last fifteen years working as a weekend mall cop. Plenty of shoplifters to catch and fights to break up. Every Monday morning, he shares stories with coworkers on his nine-to-five job. Tales of the soft underbelly of America with fleeting moments of optimism.

Greg is not a one-dimensional, comical, cardboard character cut from an episode of the Mall Cop movie. He brings to his novel over thirty years of experience from the following fields: community organizing, community development, economic development, city planning, and mental health advocacy. Greg bakes big picture themes into his novel and blogs. With a bachelor's in political science/secondary education from the Catholic University of America in Washington D.C. and a master's degree in urban planning from New York University in New York City, his writings propose outside-of-the-box solutions to vexing issues confronting society.

As the father of four who worked two and three jobs for the last thirty years, Greg grapples with issues of health insurance, college debt, and housing costs. He describes his novel Mall Child as "writings from the trenches of life". Greg encourages everyone to join him "in the trenches".